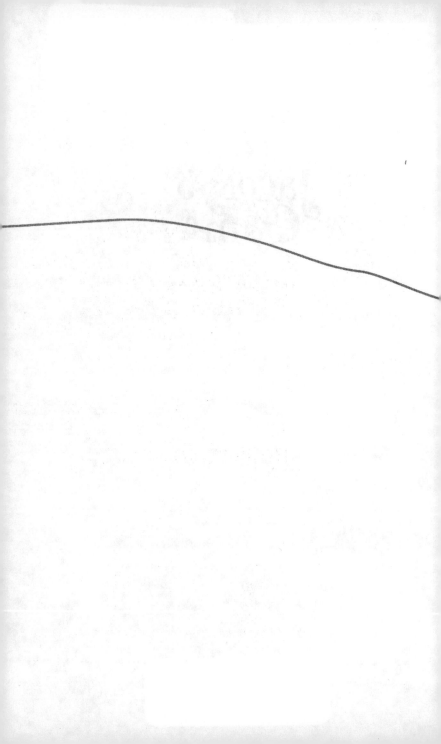

ALISON PRINCE

WALKER
BOOKS

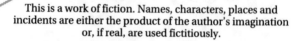

First published 2006 by Walker Books Ltd
87 Vauxhall Walk, London SE11 5HJ

2 4 6 8 10 9 7 5 3 1

Text © 2006 Alison Prince
Cover illustration © Gary Powell/Photonica/Getty Images

This book has been typeset in Utopia

Printed and bound in Great Britain by Creative Print and Design
(Wales), Ebbw Vale

British Library Cataloguing in Publication Data:
a catalogue record for this book
is available from the British Library

ISBN-13: 978-1-84428-750-5
ISBN-10: 1-84428-750-5

www.walkerbooks.co.uk

"If I wasn't real," Alice said – half-laughing through her tears, it all seemed so ridiculous – "I shouldn't be able to cry."

Through the Looking-Glass
Lewis Carroll

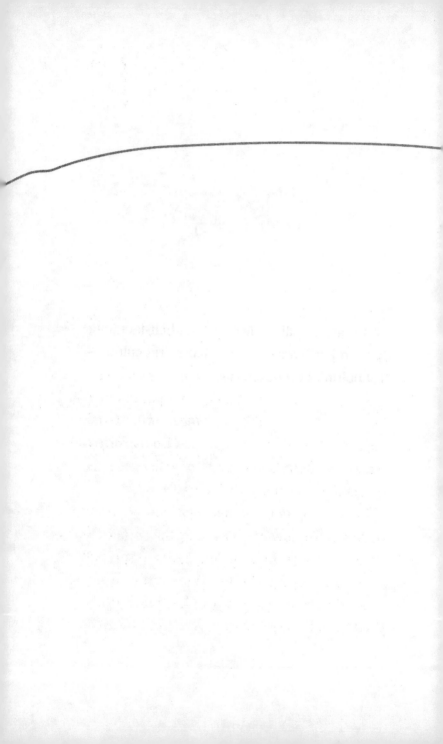

Philip is DEAD, Mum. He died eight weeks ago.

That's what I want to say. Wake her up, shake her out of it. I won't, though. No point. She'd just murmur something like, "You don't have to tell me." Then she'd open the back door and go out again. There's only one thing that interests her, and it's not me or the house.

I'm looking down at her right now from my bedroom window. She's pushing that stupid little hand mower into the long grass, push, pull back, push again. Rattle, whirr, rattle, whirr. There's a perfectly good ride-on mower in the shed – Philip used to chug up and down the lawn on it until he got ill – but she's not *mowing* the grass, nothing so simple. She's making these loopy paths in it. She says it's a labyrinth.

It was Philip's idea, of course. The last thing he bought her was a book called *World Labyrinths* – one of those glossy books with lots of photographs. I took a look at it one day when Mum was out. Most of the labyrinths it showed were made of grotty old stone in Turkey, but there were posh ones inlaid on cathedral floors, and a whole lot in people's gardens, needless to say. And dreadful ones made of beanbags in Community Centres, with people walking around in them looking spiritual. Mum looks like that these days, skin and bone and huge eyes. It makes me want to shake her.

She used to sit by Philip's bed, turning over the pages of the labyrinth book with him, talking quietly. She said his death was something they had to do together. She was sure I'd understand. I tried hard, but it went on for so *long*, and I just got sick of it. I suppose it was selfish, but I wished she could be in the kitchen sometimes when I came home from school. She never was. She hardly budged from his bedside except to get herself a herbal and refill his hot water bottle.

The crematorium had pews upholstered in red plastic that made a noise like a whoopee cushion when you sat down. There weren't any hymns, just a CD of Joan Baez singing "What Have They Done To The Rain", because Philip used to like it. Which just shows what a miserable, old-fashioned git he was.

I held Mum's hand while she cried. I knew I ought to cry as well, but I couldn't. I watched the long coffin with Philip inside it slide away through the curtains that had a hidden fire behind them, and thought, with any luck, Mum and I could be the way we were before she married him.

Some hopes. The very next day, she was pacing through the long grass with bits of stick and a big ball of string. Then she got this push mower from a jumble sale.

It's stupid to be jealous of a lawnmower, but I keep having this dream, where I'm standing in the grass and she's mowing her way towards me. *Mum,* I say in the dream, trying to sound cool and dignified. *Good morning.* (Or *afternoon,* or *evening,* according to where the sun is

9

in the sky.) *I am your daughter, Antigone, commonly known as Tig or Tiggy. Remember me?*

She smiles. *Don't be silly, darling,* she says, *of course I remember you.* But she keeps coming towards me, and I have to jump back before the whirring blades of the mower cut into my feet.

This isn't a dream, though. This is real.

I can't go on standing here, watching her. I've done it so often, it's getting to be like a tune that drives you mad. Maybe it's addictive, like smoking. There ought to be big, black letters on the window. WATCHING YOUR MOTHER CAN SERIOUSLY DAMAGE YOUR HEALTH. And anti-Mum patches to stick on your arm like the nicotine sort. Kate did patches. Not that she smoked much, but she went on a health kick and said she had to detox. She said patches were better than fags because they didn't make your hair smell of smoke.

Maybe I'll go and see Kate. Can't keep hanging around here or I'll go mad. I pick up my mobile and key in her number.

"Hi!" She sounds breathless.

"Hi Kate, it's Tig. What are you doing?"

"Playing tennis with Poppy."

"Oh, right." That's all I need.

"Why don't you come over? We're at the courts by the open-air swimming pool."

"I don't want to play tennis."

"You don't have to. There's a café here, we can have a drink. You all right? You sound a bit down."

"Yeah. Bit."

"What's the matter?"

"Oh – I don't know. Everything."

"Get yourself over here. Poppy's got to go when we've finished, but I'll hang on."

"OK. See you soon."

I'm going down the stairs, through the kitchen, out of the back door. The sun pounces on me from a blazing sky. I should have enjoyed this hot summer, but it's been horrible.

Mum's mowing, of course. She doesn't see me. Maybe I ought to say something. Make an effort.

I shout over the whirring and clattering. "HOW'S IT GOING?"

"Oh, hello, darling."

She rubs her forehead with the back of her

wrist, pushing her fair hair back from her eyes. She's wearing a white shirt of Philip's over bleached old jeans. People think it's odd, me having such a pale kind of mother when I'm so dark, but they can just mind their own business. She says, "It's quite difficult, actually. But interesting."

There's a pause. She doesn't actually start mowing again, but she's staring at the grass.

"If you want any help, you've only got to say," I tell her.

It sounds utterly insincere, which it is, of course. I don't want to help her, I want her to forget the whole stupid thing.

She's looking at me now, frowning in the sun.

"The thing is, Tiggy, it's like – well, a painting or something. A question of finding what's in your own mind. So, at this stage, I have to do it on my own."

"I see." In other words, *Get lost.*

She blunders on. "It's really nice of you to offer. Later, when the pattern's there, I'd love you to help. It's just—" She's careful what she says, knowing how I feel about Philip "—just a bit of unfinished business. I have to find my centre."

"Yes. Well, I hope you enjoy it." I turn away.

Philip will never be finished. He's like electrical impulses in a computer, he's there for ever. Delete him and he shifts to the Recycle Bin. Empty that and he's still on the hard drive, he hasn't gone. It's worse than when he was alive, he's like air, I'm taking him in with every breath. The idea makes me feel sick. I'm walking off.

"Where are you going?" Mum calls.

"To see Kate. Not that it matters."

She's left the mower, she's following me. "Tiggy, why are you so *hard*?"

I tell her over my shoulder, "If anyone's hard round here, it's not me."

"But don't you *care*, haven't you any *feeling*?"

"I asked if I could help, didn't I? What more do you want?"

"You didn't mean it. You were just being polite."

"Would you rather I was rude?"

"Don't be silly."

I've lost it completely now, hot words are pouring out of me like steam out of a kettle, I'm telling her what I think, and a whole lot more as well. I want to hack into her saintly suffering, smash up her paleness and her poetic wisps of hair, make her join me in this angry mess, because this is the way things are, it's time she got real.

She's standing there with her head down and her hands clenched at her sides, enduring the torrent of words. She doesn't attempt to answer. *Good.* I reach the back door of the garage and storm into the oily-smelling dimness. I grab my bike from where it leans beside the ride-on mower and push it out through the up-and-over door into the waiting blaze of sun.

Mum's followed me. She's standing by the car with her hand on its bonnet.

"Tig, do be careful," she says.

I slam the door down hard. It clicks home, shutting her away.

* * *

Pedalling between the leafy gardens of our road, I'm desperately wondering how I can escape. I should have gone to stay with Gran. She lives in Brighton, which is an OK place, but she's a piano teacher, and that's a bore. Pupils come to her house, and they make the same mistakes all the time – it drives me up the wall. I don't know how Gran stands it, but I suppose she needs the money.

Heat comes up off the road like a scalding radiator, and that's OK, it's great. Ordinary British weather is such rubbish, half warm and half wet, muggy all the time. I've got the right kind of skin for a hot summer, I'm smooth and brown, that's the way I was born. I don't have to slap on sun cream like Kate does. Got my genes from my dad, I suppose – they couldn't have come from my pale and irritating mother.

I swerve in through the car park and skid to a stop beside the high netting of the tennis courts. There's Kate, sitting at a table outside the café. She waves. I put the front wheel of the bike in one of the concrete slots and go to join her.

"I got you a Coke," she says, pushing a can towards me.

"Thanks."

I rip the ring pull and drink some. I don't really like Coke, but it was nice of her.

"You all right?" Kate asks.

"Yeah. Sort of."

"Trouble with your mum again?"

"She's off her head."

"Perhaps she's still upset about your dad."

"He wasn't my dad."

"No, but you know who I mean – what was his name?"

"Philip."

Philip of the pale blue eyes like a dead cod. Grey fuzz round the back of his head, bald on top through wearing that stupid wig in court.

"Who was your real father?" Kate asks. She takes another swig from her can and adds, "Don't tell me if you'd rather not."

Kate's the only person I know who could ask a question like that without blushing. I admire her for it – but I'm gobsmacked, all the same. I've never talked about him to anyone, and my lungs feel kind of jumpy at the idea of it. But why not? It can't make things any worse. I take a breath – but the words aren't there. Take another. Try again.

"His name was Lamin. Mum met him in Senegal."

"Africa. Oh, right – I always thought you were West Indian. Was your mum working there?"

"No, she was on holiday. Two weeks." I laugh before Kate does. "They didn't hang about, did they?"

Kate shrugs. "Holidays are for enjoying yourself. Does your dad still live there?"

"Far as I know, yes."

"You've never met him?"

"No."

"And you're not in touch with him?"

"No."

"Shame, really. So when did Philip turn up?"

"I was five."

And after that, Mum shared a bath with him instead of me, and locked the bathroom door. I still can't think what she saw in him. He was years older than her. He had brown liver spots on his hands, and expensive teeth. You could see gold on the inner surfaces of them when he laughed.

"You said he was a barrister." Kate still sounds casual. "He must have earned a packet."

"Absolutely pots."

"Lucky break for your mum."

And for you, she means. She thinks I'm making a fuss about nothing. My fury boils up again.

"So I'm supposed to be grateful? Well, I'm

not. I didn't ask to be given things, I didn't choose to be lucky."

"I never said—"

"I don't want to be grateful to anyone. I'd like to go and live in the streets with the homeless. If I was cold and dirty and broke, at least I wouldn't get told I'm lucky all the time."

Kate refuses to be ruffled. "Not much fun, though," she says.

Fun! What's that?

"Nothing's any fun. I'd like to blank everything out and start again. Rewrite my whole life."

"You'd have to keep the same parents though, or you wouldn't be you."

"Better if I wasn't."

"Ah, come on." She reaches out and puts her hand over mine. "I wouldn't want you any different."

I'm touched. "Honest?"

"Honest. You're all right, Tig. You're just on a bit of a downer. You need to think of one thing that would make you happy and go for it."

I know what made me happy. Or who. But he's gone. I'm scowling.

"You must be able to think of *something*,"

Kate says.

I'm not going to tell her. I've never told anyone. She goes on sitting there, looking bright
and helpful.

Oh, all right, then.

"I want Jacoby back."

"Who's Jacoby?"

"My cat. But he's dead."

"I cried for days when our dog died," Kate
says. As if Jacoby could be anything like some
grotty dog – but she doesn't know. "You should
get another one, Tig. I know it's not the same,
but—"

"Mum said she was allergic to cats. But she
was never allergic before." Now I've started
talking about it, I can't stop. "We had Jacoby
when we were on our own, and she was fine.
Then Philip came, and, about a week later,
I came back from school and Jacoby had gone.
Philip told me the vet had to put him down
because he had Feline AIDS. Then Mum said
we couldn't have another cat because she was
allergic. But it was Philip who was allergic.
Anyone with half a brain could see that – he
kept sneezing and mopping his eyes whenever

Jacoby was near. Mum took the blame because she didn't want me to hate Philip."

"But Philip's gone," Kate points out. "If that's right about him being the allergic one, you could have another cat now."

"Oh, yes," I say bitterly. "We'd hardly done with the funeral before Mum said her allergy was better, so would I like a cat."

Kate shrugs. "Well, then." *No problem*, she means. She just doesn't get it.

"Mum *lied* to me," I shout at her. "She took Philip's side, did whatever he told her. *Joy, darling, that cat really will have to go.* So Joy darling took Jacoby to the vet and had him killed. I can't forgive her."

Jacoby was special. He was black, with yellow eyes and a long, aristocratic nose. He had thick fur and a feathery tail like a squirrel. He was always there when I needed him. He was my friend. I'll never have another friend like him.

"You have to move on," Kate says.

"I don't *want* to move on. I want things to be the way they were."

"But time goes forward," she says patiently. "You're stuck with it. We all are."

I prop my elbows on the arms of the white plastic chair so my shoulders hunch up.

"I don't want to go forward. I want to go back and back and back. I don't care how far back."

I'd like to be unborn. I'd like to be nothing.

Kate shakes her head. "Things are fixed. It's a shame about your cat, but you've got to be reasonable."

Be reasonable. That's what Philip always said.

I'm up out of my chair, almost tipping the table over. Kate makes a grab for her can, and rescues it. Mine rolls off the edge. The brown, fizzy liquid is running out across the concrete slabs.

I'm cycling fast, sun blazing in front of me. South, I'm going south. I won't stop until I get to Brighton. Fifty miles, but so what? I can do that. I'll phone Gran, tell her I'm coming. The heat is ferocious, melting the tarmac, there's sweat running down my face, I can't see where I'm going for the sun's dazzle. My front wheel almost touches the rear doors of a van – jam the brakes on, swerve a bit, stick my foot down on the road. Traffic lights, we're all stopped.

21

I get my mobile out of my pocket, look down at it for Gran's number, thumb it in.

We're moving again. There's traffic all round me, diesel fumes making my eyes run. I'm cycling one-handed, listening to the number ringing in Brighton. *Tig, do be careful.* Mum would have kittens if she could see me now.

Kittens. Cats. Jacoby.

Dual carriageway coming up. Good. If I'm going faster it'll stop me thinking.

You must be joking, says Jacoby in my mind. *You'll always think.*

With my mobile to my ear, I glance over my right shoulder, see the gap and swerve into it. Really moving now, up off the saddle, leaning forward so the wind blows down the front of my T-shirt, single hand in the centre of the handle-bars, phone still ringing. I'm balanced, I'm OK, this is good. The voice in my ear is close and tiny in the traffic –

THE PERSON YOU ARE CALLING IS UN-AVAILABLE, PLEASE LEAVE A MESSAGE AFTER THE TONE.

Rats. She'll be teaching some horrible kid, I suppose. Can't send her a text while I'm on the bike, it'll have to be verbal.

"Gran," I shout, "it's me, Tig. I'm coming to see you. I'll be there in—" How long will it take? Don't know.

At least four hours, Jacoby tells me. *If you make it, which I doubt.*

THERE HE IS!

Right in front of me, black fur, fluffy tail, he's running between the traffic, I'm on top of him, he's going to be killed, *brake, BRAKE!*

I'm skidding, lost it, the bike's going sideways, shit, there's a bus—

"That was silly," Jacoby remarks.

I don't know what he means, but then, I've never quite known, and it doesn't matter. I stroke the top of his head. The sun is slanting in quiet squares across the carpet. The lawn is velvety green outside the French windows. It smells fresh-mown.

Jacoby's eyes are as yellow as ever, and his whiskers are still tapering and beautiful, standing out on either side of his long nose. I'm so glad he's not dead.

Why did I think he was dead? That's nonsense – it must have been one of my dreams. Mum says I used to have nightmares when I was small.

"I must say, it's nice to see you," says Jacoby. "Even if it was silly."

What's he nagging about? It's all very well for him, all he has to do is eat and sleep and amuse himself. "I've had a lot on my mind," I tell him, though I'm not sure what.

"Well, you haven't now," he says.

That seems to be true. I feel strangely light and empty. If I had a dream, it's gone. I frown, trying to drag it back – and in the next moment I gasp.

The pain is terrible. Every breath hurts.

"I wouldn't go there if I were you," says Jacoby. "It's not very nice at the moment."

He's obviously right. But – go where? What is it? Very cautiously, I explore again – and gasp as the pain hits me even harder.

It's very hot. I'm frantic about Jacoby, so frantic that I scream out.

"It's no use blaming me," Jacoby says.

I know I've made a small noise, I can feel the effort of it in my throat. "I'm not blaming you," I tell him. "I was just trying to work out what happened."

25

"It won't do you any good." He inspects his left paw and starts to wash it.

I need to be logical. I've had a dream, but I'm out of it now. This is real. Tall spikes of evening primrose grow in the border by the fence, I can see their floppy, pale yellow flowers that last for just a single day. The ones further down the stalk are withered and brown, rather a mess, really. Jacoby is sitting on the windowsill, and my hand is reaching out to stroke his fur. Its softness is lovely.

"Thank you," he says, standing up and arching his back. "That's very pleasant."

"I thought you were dead," I say. "But you're not, are you?"

"Not at the moment." He sits down again and goes on washing.

I start to ask what he means, but the door opens and Philip comes in. He glances at Jacoby then frowns at me.

"I've told you before," he says, "I will *not* have that cat in the sitting room. It's unhygienic."

His pale blue eyes have started to water. He pulls a folded handkerchief from his top pocket, shakes it out irritably and blows his nose.

"The cat's in the garden, *actually*," I point out.

Jacoby is outside, sitting on the shed, which has a pink rose growing over it.

Philip goes on glaring at me.

"You, madam, need to learn some manners," he says. He doesn't glance out to see that what I've told him is true, just turns and walks out of the room. The door bangs behind him.

Jacoby stares down at me from the shed roof. The pink roses are very beautiful against his blackness.

Philip is planning something, I know he is. It's to do with Jacoby.

There was something awful.

No, that's ridiculous. Things that haven't happened can't be remembered.

"They can, actually," Jacoby remarks.

"That's nonsense," I argue. "If a thing hasn't occurred, then it doesn't exist. So you can't remember it. Right?"

"Wrong," says Jacoby. He rubs his whiskers briskly. "It all depends where you put yourself. If you've been ahead of where we are now –

which you have – you'll come back with memories of things that haven't happened here yet. Like going to Australia, only more so."

I'm frowning. "But now is now."

He smiles his cat smile at me. "Are you sure?"

"Yes."

I put my hand on the dry wood of the shed, feeling its warmth. The rusty head of a nail sticks out just by my thumb, and there are green plastic twist-ties holding the rose stems to wires. "This is real," I say. "It's now."

"Or so you believe," says Jacoby.

His yellow eyes are staring down into mine. I can see the black fur on his face, short and close round his nose and his neat mouth. If I can't believe this, what can I believe?

"You were upset about something," he reminds me. "Do you know what it was? Be careful," he adds, and I know why. Pain and panic are lurking out there.

"It was a dream," I say. "Wasn't it?"

He gives a purr of amusement. "There you are, you see," he says. "It was real at the time, and now you think it can't be, just because you're stuck with the idea that there's only one Now."

I frown. There's something wrong with this argument, but I can't work out what it is. Jacoby's given up bothering. He stands up and stretches.

"Anyway," he says, "what would you like to do?"

"You mean right now?"

"Yes. Or whatever we agree to call it."

"I don't know. What *can* I do?"

"Anything you like."

"You're joking."

"No," he says mildly. "I thought you might like to go somewhere, since you're here."

Go somewhere.

Gran, I'm going to see Gran.

There's a little fountain between the ferns in her shady back garden.

"Splendid," says Jacoby. "Go and see your gran."

We are walking on the Downs, high above the sea. The long grass swishes against my legs.

"France is over there," Gran says. "It's not far."

The misty blueness ends in a straight line where the sky starts. There's no sign of France.

"You could see it if the earth was flat," Gran goes on. "It's just over the edge. Closer to us than London."

"Weird."

France seemed much further away when I went with Mum and Philip in the car. Flat fields and poplar trees, bars of black-white shadow across the roads. War cemeteries with neat rows of white stones. Horrible places, they gave me the creeps.

"Would it be a bore if I sat down for a rest?" Gran asks. "My silly old legs."

I sit beside her in the long grass. Her ankles are swollen, bulging over the straps of her sandals, and a purple network of veins discolours the skin. I glance at them, then look away. I'm not bored, just a bit sad. Why do old people have to get ugly? Perhaps it's so they won't mind too much when they die.

I don't want Gran to die. I lie back and stare at the sky. Fluffy clouds are moving against the deep blue, and I feel as if the earth is tipping down towards the sea, like when you're on a Ferris wheel, falling forward into nowhere so your stomach lurches.

* * *

"That was nice, wasn't it," says Jacoby.

He's sprawled on the branch of a tree, looking smug. What's he got to be smug about? Visiting Gran was his suggestion, OK, but he didn't make it happen. It was just a scrap of something I remembered.

"Are you sure you remembered it?" he asks.

"Yes."

No. I'm not sure at all. Did I ever walk on the Downs with Gran, just the two of us?

"I knew you'd like it," Jacoby says. "Going back is such a good game."

Game? Cats don't play games.

"Yes, we do. All the time. Catching leaves, seeing off other cats, watching mouse holes. It's our form of work, but it comes to the same thing."

"Huh?"

"If you want to be happy," he says patiently, "you must find a game that you really enjoy, and work very hard at playing it. If you're busy and interested, then you're happy."

It's hopeless trying to argue with him – he's always got some smart answer.

"OK," I say. "So what are the rules of this game?"

"There aren't any. Be what you like. Go where you like and when you like." He eyes me thoughtfully. "Correct me if I'm wrong," he adds, "but you've been somewhat fed-up lately. You told your friend you'd like to delete everything and start again."

"What friend?"

"She was playing tennis. Careful," he adds. "Don't go rushing back there."

Tennis? Perhaps he means Kate – she's into tennis. But how does he know? Jacoby's never mixed with my friends. He couldn't. There's something totally wrong with the idea, like putting the moon in a bowl of eggs.

"You said you wanted to go back to a time when things were better. Back and back and back, you said. You didn't care how far. Well, that's the game. Go back to another place and time, see if you like it better."

"Is it dangerous?" I ask.

He smiles down at me from his pattern of roses and sunshine, and says, "Everything is dangerous."

"Not if you're really careful."

"*Specially* if you're careful. If you get too safe, your brain dies. They should put risk in the drinking water, like that stuff they have for your teeth."

I laugh. "Fluoride." Suddenly I'm reckless. "Go on, then – how do we start?"

"It's your choice. What's your favourite thing?"

"Shopping," I say a bit wildly. "Let's go shopping. Shall we go now?"

"Not *we*," says Jacoby. "*You.* I'm a cat, remember. Cats don't shop."

Panic. Do I have to play this game on my own?

"I'll be around," he concedes. "Probably. But take a friend if you like."

Friends. Yes, I've got lots of friends. What are their names? For some stupid reason, I've forgotten. The only one I can remember is Kate.

Jacoby sharpens his claws on the green bark of his branch.

"Kate will do," he says. "She'll be there."

He's climbing further up. I can't see him against the glittering light through the leaves.

He's gone.

We're in a café called La Scala. Kate says it's her favourite place. It's very modern, with big plants growing all over the window, and a Gaggia hissing steam.

We've had tagliatelle verde off sage green oval plates, same colour as the pasta, and the waitress has just brought coffee in little cups. It's very strong. Kate lights a cigarette. She pushes the packet across the table to me, but I shake my head. I like the idea of smoking – dead sophisticated. But whenever I try it, my eyes run and I get a coughing fit.

"Does your mother say you mustn't?" Kate asks.

She's wearing green eye shadow with glittery bits in it, and lots of black mascara. Her nails are varnished green, too.

"It's nothing to do with my mother." But it is, of course. Mum would go mad if I smoked.

"She doesn't like you wearing make-up, either, does she?"

I try not to blush. How does Kate know this?

"She's old-fashioned, that's all," I say. "She thinks anything more than powdering your nose is sinful."

"I can see."

Kate's not much older than me, but there are times when she's so superior, I wonder why I'm friendly with her. And it's not as if I don't make an effort – I bought a lipstick last week, California Dawn, my first one ever. I put some on in the bus, coming here. Is she impressed? No.

She puts her hand over mine.

"Tell you what," she says. "When we've finished this, we'll go in the Ladies and I'll do your make-up properly."

It's only a small room and there are no chairs or

anything, just the toilet and a wash basin with a mirror over it.

"Close your eyes," Kate orders. She smoothes shadow on my eyelids. "Keep them closed." I can feel the drag of a liner pencil. Mascara next. She spits on the narrow cake of it so as to get enough blackness on the little brush. I don't mind having Kate's spit on my eyes. I'm a doll in her hands. She makes me feel all warm and cared for.

"Head back," she instructs. "Don't blink."

I stand very still. It's the least I can do if she's going to make me beautiful.

"OK, now you can open them."

My face in the mirror amazes me. I'm gazing out of huge, dark eyes like a deer. Or like wonderful Audrey Hepburn, who is the best film star ever. Kate's used a dark mauve shadow, not her green one.

"Violet's right for you," she says, head on one side like an artist considering a picture.
"Goes with your colouring. That lipstick's hopeless, though. Can you wipe it off?" She rummages in her handbag. "This'll be better, you'll like it. Sugar Love."

I grab some toilet paper and remove the hopeless California Dawn.

"Part your lips," Kate instructs. "Stretch them a bit – that's right." The touch of the lipstick is cool and firm. "Now rub them together. Good."

Sugar Love is a pale pinky-mauve. It's so much lighter than my coffee-coloured skin, it's made me into a photographic negative, and my black-rimmed eyes look simply enormous. I stare at myself again, drooping my lashes like Kate does. The image glancing back from the glass is incredibly seductive. I can't believe it's me.

"Right," says Kate. She drops the lipstick back in her bag. "Let shopping commence."

I'm following her through this big store. We're in Costume Jewellery, on the ground floor. The air is hot and perfumed. Maybe they put scent in the ventilation system. It might reek of sweaty people otherwise.

Mum made me wear my school mac this morning, in case it rained, but I've taken it off and slung it over my shoulder. I feel great, as if I'm someone else. Someone worth looking at.

I always thought I was just a skinny kid, but

yesterday a girl in my form called Cara said, "Aren't you slim!" And slim is different from skinny. Cara's a real roly-poly, so I suppose almost everyone seems slim to her, but it was nice of her to say it. She's the sort who cares about how people feel. Caring Cara. I ought to be like that, but I'm not, really.

There are narrow mirrors on the pillars in between counters, and I keep glimpsing this slim girl in her black top and ballet-length skirt. It's turquoise, cinched in with a wide elastic belt. There was such a fuss when I wore that belt at school. They said it wasn't an Approved Article of Uniform, and made me take it off. Then Poppy turned up in shoes with pointy toes, and they were so busy objecting to that, they stopped noticing my elastic belt, and everyone started wearing them. I hate school, it's like being in a long tunnel with only a spot of light at the end, which is when I can leave.

Kate and I are going dancing tonight, at the Roxy. I'll go back to hers afterwards. Sometimes she stays the night at mine, but I don't like that so much. Kate's mum is often out when we get back from dancing, because she and her friend

Pam are mad about the cinema, and they go and have a drink afterwards. Make a night of it, as she says. Kate's dad is usually down the pub, playing darts. When he comes in he has a cup of tea and watches telly for a bit, then he goes to bed. He's not much bothered about us, which is great.

I love dancing. It would be so great to be flung around by a guy in a black roll-neck sweater like in *Rock Around the Clock*. I always dance near the band if I can, in case they notice me and I get discovered and appear on telly. Just a dream, of course, but—

Kate's going up the escalator. I put my foot on the sliding treads and follow her, rising above the counters and display cabinets to Ladies' Fashions.

There she is, flicking through long-sleeved tops on a rail, red Alice band on her curly hair. It used to be straight, but she got it permed for her birthday. Funny, really. I want to get mine straightened.

"These are dead expensive," she says over her shoulder. "They're much cheaper in the market. I'd have bought one last week, only I'd run out of money."

She's always running out of money – the minute she's got it, she spends it. I try not to spend more than I can help. I know it's stupid, but it's Philip's money, not mine. Perhaps that's why I like Kate. She doesn't care whose money it is. She doesn't care about anything.

We're moving from stall to stall in the crowded market, working our way round people who stop to haggle over a pair of socks or a saucepan or a bunch of carrots. The kids are eating candyfloss, some of the adults as well. There's a guy with a machine, making the stuff. He's reaching down into the whizzing drum with a long stick, twirling the pink wisps round until they build up to the size of a back-brushed hairdo. As soon as he holds up a finished head of floss, somebody buys it.

"Do you want one?" Kate asks me.

"No, thanks."

I don't like candyfloss, it only tastes of sugar, and sugar makes you fat. I thought the Sugar Love lipstick might taste sweet, but it doesn't – just a bit greasy.

There's a stall selling tools next to the candyfloss man. Sets of spanners in blue plastic cases, screwdrivers, soldering irons, electric drills. Men glance at the stuff as if they're not interested, but most of them stop to turn things over, and a good few find something they like, and dig in their pockets for money.

Dozens of people are staring up at the high counter on an open-sided lorry where a couple of butchers in striped aprons are selling meat. It looks like a huge-scale Punch and Judy show, lights above them shining down. One of the men is shouting through a microphone.

"Not six shillings, ladies and gents, not even five and sixpence, not even five bob. Four-and-six I'm asking for your prime shoulder steak." He piles slab after slab of meat onto the paper spread on his outstretched hand, then slaps it on the scale and stares at it incredulously. "Two and a half pounds of prime steak there. Two and a half pounds! And it's yours for four bob. Who's first?"

Hands are up. "Over here!" a woman shouts. She's shoving her way to the stall, digging in her purse.

41

The man wraps the meat and hands it down to her. I'm glad I'm not a housewife, lugging home two and a half pounds of dead cow. I don't eat meat. At least, I don't if I think about it. I suppose there must have been mince in the tagliatelle sauce, but it's different if it's Italian. I didn't eat all of it, anyway. Kate finished mine.

She's found the clothes stall.

Her hands are on her hips, she's staring at the striped tops on their hangers. They're green and black, black and white, pink and grey, lemon and blue, orange and white – but she's not pleased.

"Haven't you got red and white?" she asks the man. "You had last week."

"Sorry, love. How about orange?" He unhooks one and offers it. "Suits you a treat. Just your colour."

"No, it's not," she says.

The man hangs it up again.

Kate glances at me and says, "I might get a black one like yours. There's a nice one up there with a slash neck."

She never said she liked my black top. I feel really pleased.

The man gets it down for her and she holds it up against herself.

"Seven-and-six is too much," she says.

"Six bob, then," he says.

"Can't you make it five?"

"You'll have me in the poor house. Five-and-six, and that's my last word. Take it or leave it." He's going to hang the top up again.

Kate takes it.

We're moving on.

"You haven't bought anything," Kate says. "Can't you find what you want?"

"I expect I'll see something," I tell her.

"Hope so," says Kate. "It's awful to go home with nothing new."

We're walking past a stall piled with soft toys. Dogs with brown patches, puppies with pink felt tongues, teddy bears, white rabbits, cats in three colours, brown and orange and black—

Black cat.

I stop and stare. That's what I want.

"Don't be silly," Jacoby says in my ear. "They're not real."

"Yes, they are."

"What are?" asks Kate.

I'd forgotten she was there. "I meant, they're not real *animals*. But they are real toys."

She shrugs and gives me a funny look. Stupid of me to speak aloud.

Jacoby is holding out one of the black cats. No, it's not Jacoby, it's the stallholder. It's just that he's black – I got confused for a moment.

"Very nice," the man says, smiling. "Very soft. Feel." He holds the cat out to me. The palms of his hands are pale on the insides, same as mine are.

The cat has plush fur, but that's the only soft thing about it. Inside, it's filled with something stiff and crunchy, like straw. Its amber eyes are made of glass, and one of them is coming loose on its metal pin. I hand it back and shake my head. The stallowner's eyes are as amber as the cat's, very tigerish in his dark face, but his smile has shifted.

"You too big for toys, girl," he says. "You lookin' for the real thing."

"Come on," says Kate.

Her hand tightens on my arm, she's walking me past the stall. I can feel the man still looking at my swinging skirt and my slim waist. He whistles after me, and I glance back at him out of my huge eyes. He raises his chin a little and pushes his lips together, blowing me a kiss.

"He's horrible," says Kate.

"No, he's not."

I don't know why I say this. It's just that he was black.

"You're the sort who'll end up getting murdered in a ditch," Kate is scolding. "You've got no sense."

"I have got sense," I tell her. "I sense all sorts of things."

"That's different."

"How is it different?"

"Don't be stupid," she says. "Sensing things means looking at them and hearing them and smelling them."

"Not necessarily."

This is the kind of argument I have with Jacoby. I love it, but Kate doesn't.

"Oh, come on, Tig. When I talk about sense, I mean being sensible."

I know that, of course, but I keep arguing.

"If you're sensible you have to decide what's

best, right? And how can you know what's best unless you've sensed how things are? You can't make a proper choice unless you've tried every-thing."

"Good point," Jacoby says in my ear.

"That's why you'll end up in a ditch," says Kate. "You'd stand there looking at some dread-ful bloke and thinking about choices, and never notice he's going to strangle you."

"I think I might notice, actually."

"No, you wouldn't. Half the time you don't see what's obvious, you're off on some batty idea of your own."

I shrug and give up.

Kate pauses at a stall that sells bracelets and necklaces made of beads, but I drift on, think-ing about the tiger-man and his soft toys. *The real thing.* He was talking about sex, of course.

The women round the butcher's stall have all had sex. That's why they're standing there with heavy plastic bags cutting into their fingers, holding up the money for two and a half pounds of steak. Sex makes families, and fami-lies are heavy. Once you've got them, you have to lug home meat and toilet rolls and tins of beans and pounds of potatoes and big packets of washing powder. If the tiger-man thinks I want to carry all that weight of cubs and their meat and nappies and pushchairs, he's wrong.

"That's logical," Jacoby remarks. "If you rule out the things you don't want, you'll come to what you do want." Then he adds, "That's the point of the game, if you remember."

The game.

"The go back game," he says.

It means something, and the meaning is growing larger and closer. In another instant, I'll tip over into some kind of dream that I share with Jacoby, slide away into some other place. It's all gone strange. I'm feeling sick and dizzy. I stare hard at a cabbage leaf on the dirty cobbles. I'm not sure if it's real.

Kate is running to catch me up.

"I bought five of them," she says, "look!" She holds up her wrist, rattling her new bead bracelets, mauve and blue, pink and turquoise and green. I focus on them carefully. They are threaded on fine elastic. There are freckles on the back of Kate's pale hand. These things must be real. I start to feel better.

Kate gives me a twist of newspaper.

"This one's for you," she says.

Squidging it gently between my fingers, I can feel the beads inside.

"Oh, Kate, that's so kind."

I'm afraid I won't like it. I hate pink and green and blue.

But the bracelet is red and amber, with tiny white beads between dark brown ones. I slip it on my wrist. I do like it. Very much.

This man can dance. He can really dance, we're utterly together in this pounding music. I'm part of the drumming, part of the coloured lights, I'm everywhere, I'm hurling over his shoulder, the ceiling and floor flash past and I'm on my feet again, still in the rhythm. He's chewing gum, dead casual, he doesn't even look at me but his grip is strong, I can depend on him. We're doing this so well, we don't have to smile, just stay with it, concentrate, be easy. People have stopped to look at us, we've got a space of our own in a circle of watchers.

The number ends. I'm sweating, but I feel wonderful. A few people applaud us, but they've turned away now, everyone's surging towards the stage, girls are screaming, reaching up towards the band. I'm screaming too, stretching my arms up like they do. We'd grab hold of the players if we could, we'd eat them, we so much want to be part of them.

They start a new number. Where's the guy I was dancing with? I can't see him anywhere.

There he is, with a girl in an off-the-shoulder yellow dress. She's the film-star sort with fluffy blonde hair. I hate her. She doesn't dance as well as me, he's stupid to have picked her. I'm standing here alone, the floor's crowded with couples and I'm getting in everyone's way. I want to dance, I can't bear to walk off to that stupid table where I parked a glass of lemonade ages ago. I don't care what people think, I'll dance on my own.

A man is pushing his way between the couples, coming towards me. He grabs my hand, hauls me close. He's quite old, nearly forty perhaps, very thin and bony. He puts his arm round my waist and starts some sort of stupid quickstep – he's not into rock at all.

"What's your name?" he asks.

He's holding me too tight. I try to make a bit of space between us, but his arm tightens its grip.

"Come on, darling, what's your name?" he repeats. He's spinning me round, the mirror ball is sending specks of light leaping along the pink walls.

I say the first name that comes into my head.

"Cara." Don't I know someone called Cara?

The man laughs. His breath smells of something strong – whisky, is it?

"Italian for *darling*," he says. "Or Spanish or something. You Spanish? You look as if you might be." He tries some sort of tango move, then goes back to his rhythmless quickstep. His foot kicks into my ankle. "I'm Gordon," he says. "Come here often, do you?"

I don't know if I come here often. Gordon's hand is on my bottom, bony fingers digging into my flesh, pressing me closer against him.

Kate dances by with a round-faced boy in glasses, and I make a desperate face at her. She gets the point at once.

"Powder room!" she shouts.

Brilliant.

"'Scuse me a minute," I say to Gordon.

His grip doesn't relax, so I say it again, louder.

"EXCUSE ME!"

He grins and says, "What for? Done something naughty, have you?"

"I need to go to the Ladies."

"Can't it wait?"

"No."

"Ah, come on."

I try to push him away, but he's horribly strong. In the next minute I'm fighting like a mad thing, screaming at him, hitting him. He puts an arm up to defend himself and loses his balance. He's cannoned into another couple, and the man he's collided with grabs him and starts shouting. I'm pushing between the dancers to get away, someone yells at me, but I keep going.

The door of the powder room closes behind me, deadening the music. Its walls are papered with purple flowers, and it smells of disinfectant and stale perfume. I thought it was nice when Kate and I first came in, but now it looks tacky.

"You wanted to come here," Jacoby points out. "You were enjoying it."

"I *know*. Don't start."

"I'm not starting," he says mildly.

This is not the time for arguing. I just want him to be warm and furry and comfortable. I need him.

"I'm only trying to find a place you like," he points out. "That's the game, if you remember. Going back to find somewhere nicer."

I don't want to remember. I don't want to play any stupid game.

A worse thought comes. *Perhaps I actually AM playing it.* If that's right, how do I stop? What am I supposed to do?

"Don't worry," Jacoby says. "This day will end. All days do."

"At midnight, you mean? Glass slipper time?"

He doesn't seem to know about glass slippers. "When you go to sleep."

"Because sleep divides one day from the next?"

"Actually," he says with precision, "it's a dream that does the dividing. Catnaps are nice, but they're too short for dreams, you wake up in the same day."

I nod, but I don't want to talk about catnaps.

"Jacoby, you've got to tell me. Is this a dream?"

He looks away for a moment, then back. "That's the easiest way to think of it," he says.

We stare at each other. The centres of his eyes are wide and dark.

"I don't understand," I tell him. And I am so lost that I bury my face in his black fur for comfort. His purring warmth surrounds me. For a minute or two, it's enough – but a new fear jabs at me.

"You will be there, won't you? In these dreams or whatever they are?"

"Yes," he says. "I'll always be there. It's where I belong."

Kate bursts into the powder room as if blown through the door by the gale of applause and screaming outside.

"Sorry," she gasps." Couldn't get away till the music stopped. That guy you were dancing with looked a real creep."

"Too right."

"Won't be a moment." She goes into one of the cubicles.

I stare at my dark eyes in the mirror. I can't

see Jacoby. But he was here. *It's where I belong.* Behind me, the purple-flowered walls are reflected. Surely this is real? But how can I know?

The toilet flushes and Kate comes out.

"Are you upset?" she asks. "Do you want to go home, or shall we stay a bit longer?"

This day will end. All days do.

"May as well keep going."

"OK," says Kate. "But watch out who you dance with, right?"

"Yes."

"You sure you're OK?" I'm not sure of anything, but I nod. And we go out again, into the music.

We make them do encores, but at last it's all over and the crowd goes pouring out into the street. There are a couple of heavies in evening dress chatting to each other at the door, not much bothered to look out for trouble now the gig's over. One of them has a squashed-looking nose, like a boxer. The other is taller, a strong-looking man with receding hair. He is wearing dark glasses, and as I pass him he takes them off and wipes his pale blue eyes with a white handkerchief. I have seen him before, but I don't know where. For some reason, I am afraid of him.

He looks at me, but his face is expressionless. He replaces his dark glasses, and seems blind again – unless I am the blind one.

"Spoilt brats, this lot," he says to the squashed-nose man. "There was a time when kids were kids. Went on being kids until they left school and got a job. They call themselves teenagers now – neither one thing nor the other. The way they carry on, you'd think they're new and wonderful."

Squashed-nose laughs.

"New, all right," he says. "The new big spenders. Records, clothes, magazines, all that stuff. Great for the suppliers. See teenagers, see profit."

Dark-glasses shrugs and says, "At least they're providing a bit of business. I can't see what use they are otherwise, hanging around in flared jeans with their hair too long. At their age, I had to get out and work. Still do. Telephone operator all day, bouncer at night. Seeing myself though night school."

"What d'you hope to get out of it?"

"Law degree. Money. Respect. You name it."

He wipes his eyes again.

"I think he may sense that I'm here," Jacoby murmurs, very close beside me. "He's allergic to cats." And I know the man's name.

Philip.

PHILIP.

I'm somewhere else. French windows, squares of sunshine, a rose tree—

"Tig!" Kate shouts. "Come *on,* we've got to get the bus."

She's staring back at me from the bottom of the steps. I go to join her. My legs feel strangely wobbly.

"Sorry," I say. "It was just – someone I thought I knew."

"Not one of the bouncers? Honestly, what are you like?"

We start out along the pavement. Behind me, the man called Philip reaches up for the steel shutter above the double doors of the Roxy. He pulls it down with a sharp rattle and clicks the padlock home.

4

I can't breathe properly. There's something blocking my nose and the back of my throat, *I can't swallow …*

Everything hurts…

The hurt is too much, I can't bear it, I'm breaking in pieces. A voice has started to make a noise about it, perhaps it's my voice, I don't know. It's a kind of scream but it's spluttery, like someone choking.

NURSE, a voice calls, NURSE. Someone gets up from beside me. She's running to the door, still shouting.

I've floated away. It's better up here. Looking down at the room is quite interesting. People

57

have come in, they're bending over a bed with a pink cover. The girl in the bed has a tube coming out of her nose. Her hair is dark against the pillow.

I've never seen things in this way before, from above. It's nice, just floating. Very easy. A nurse is rubbing the girl's arm with cotton wool soaked with something from a bottle, she's slipping in the needle of a syringe, pressing the plunger home. I think I can feel it … no, I can't. I don't feel anything.

The girl who is me is going to sleep, her voice is fading, she's not making the noise any more.

Let go, float away.

Away …

I was dreaming about something very weird. Bright lights, a hospital or something. It's not bright here in Kate's room, the curtains are drawn across so there's just a brown glow from the street lamps outside. My bed is quite close to Kate's, almost near enough to put my hand on. The sound of someone snoring comes through the wall. It's probably her dad. Kate's mum looks so neat and precise, I'm sure she wouldn't snore.

"The man in dark glasses," says Jacoby, "You know who he was, don't you?"

"Um – hang on." I can't quite remember.

"Outside the dance hall," Jacoby says patiently. "He pulled the shutter down. Philip. You know him."

"No, I don't."

"You do. It's just that you don't want to."

"Oh, shut up."

The hot-water bottle Kate's mum gave me has gone cold now. It feels disgusting, like a dead slug. I haul it out and put it on the floor. Jacoby is sitting there, looking perfectly calm.

"You've done it again," I say. "Haven't you?"

"Done what?"

"Just – arrived. As if it's perfectly normal."

"It *is* perfectly normal."

"No, it's not. You can't appear in different places whenever you want, like the cat in *Alice in Wonderland* – what was it called?"

"Cheshire. A distant relative of mine. Why can't I?"

"That's not the way things work. When people go away, they walk out of the door or drive off in a car or something. They tell you where

59

they're going. They don't just vanish and turn up somewhere else."

"They might if you weren't noticing."

"I *was* noticing! I always notice."

"That's all right, then. You'll get used to it."

"I don't want to get used to it, I want to understand."

He rubs behind his ear absently and says, "It's layers, you see."

"Layers?" For a mad moment, I think he means chickens.

"Layers of time," he explains. "All stacked in a pile, most recent at the top."

"Like pancakes."

"If you say so. The point is, you can go up and down through these layers as you wish. The one we are in at the moment got put on the pile about forty years ago."

"You're joking."

"No," he says mildly.

Things seem to be turning somersaults in my head. Forty years *ago*. What does he mean, *ago?* Ago from when?

"Where's the real now?" I ask him. "Where have I come from?"

He jumps up from the floor and settles beside my pillow, so his dark fur blots out everything else.

"You've just looked at the real now," he says, "and it isn't much fun at the moment. I should stay here if I were you."

"But—"

He reaches out a long paw and places it on the tip of my nose.

"Do stop trying to be reasonable."

I laugh.

"Antigone, for goodness' sake, be reasonable," Miss Webb says. "What is the formula for quadratics?"

I don't understand what quadratics are. They sound like people in wheelchairs.

Room 23 is full of the scent of cut grass, because Mr Sprocket is driving the gang mower across the field. There are two sets of blades in the middle and two on each side, and they can be folded up when he's not using it.

"Look – in – your – book," Miss Webb says through clenched teeth. "It's all there, in black and white."

I'm turning the pages over. They've all got the same pattern, with rows of numbers and chunks of text. I don't know which one she wants, I can't do this, I can't see it, a formula doesn't have a look of its own like a chair or a rabbit or a daisy, I don't know what she means, I've never known. I'm not going to cry, I don't cry any more because I know I'm hopeless so I've given up, she can do what she likes, but I mustn't cry, I mustn't cry.

She's running her fingers through her hair. It's grey hair like wire wool only not rusty. Mum uses wire wool for saucepans, and it's rusty, it makes an orange puddle in the soap dish.

Miss Webb sighs and gives up. "Somebody tell her."

People laugh. They've all got their hands up except the really thick ones like Maisie Adams. I'm not like Maisie Adams, I'm *not*.

I'd like to drive a gang mower. I like the way the cloud of grass kicks up behind it. I love the smell.

"You're not being asked to *understand*," says Philip. "Just do what you are told. Apply the formula, and it will give you the answer to the problem. That's easy enough, isn't it?"

I nod my head because he expects me to.

"Right. Now, show me the formula for quadratic equations."

There's a curl of pencil-sharpening on the kitchen table. It's got red edges because the pencil it came from had red paint on the outside. I press it gently with my finger, and it changes into a little mess of wood powder.

"I give up," Philip says. He pushes his chair back, scraping it hard across the floor.

He doesn't bother to shut the door to the sitting room, so I can hear what he says to Mum.

"I've never met anyone so obstinate. She simply refuses to be reasonable."

"Well done," Jacoby says. "Two more layers, just like that. I knew you could do it if you didn't try."

That's nonsense, but never mind. The main thing is, I'm back here. I've been to a worrying place, but it's all right now. I can feel the warm weight of the bedclothes and of my beloved cat curled beside me. Things don't get more real than this.

"Don't be too sure," murmurs Jacoby.

* * *

I love the scent of mown grass.

I'm staring out of my bedroom window. Mum's down there, pushing a clattering little hand mower into the lawn that's as long as hay now.

Damn, *damn*—

NO!

I'm awake again, gasping as if I'd been dunked in cold water.

Jacoby's yellow eyes are staring into mine, but I'm scared. For a moment, I've been some-one else. Someone so charged with pain and fury, I don't know how she could live. Was that girl really me?

"Yes, she was," Jacoby says. "She is." After a pause, he adds, "It may be that she *won't* live. It depends what you decide."

"No! I can't be responsible for someone else!"

"She's not someone else, Tiggy. She's you." The tips of his claws just prick my skin, to make sure I'm listening. "You know that, don't you?"

And I do, of course. I can't hide anything from those yellow eyes.

"So you are responsible," he goes on. "But there's no hurry. She'll wait."

"What do I have to do, though? How *long* will she wait?"

"For as long as it takes."

It's a worrying idea, but Jacoby doesn't seem worried. He's curled himself up and closed his eyes. I'm trying to understand how things fit together, but I can't.

After a bit, I say, "It's all to do with these layers, isn't it?"

"Yes," says Jacoby.

"Can't I see it all together? Like, from outside, so I know where I am?"

"No. One thing at a time."

"But I want to know where I am. Whether it's real or not."

He yawns. "It's real while it's happening," he says.

His sleepiness is washing over me, as if I'm floating in a warm tide.

"Mixed up," I manage to say. *I'm so mixed up.*

And in a dream, there's a dish of catfood on the floor, peas and prawns mixed. Jacoby never liked the peas.

"**G**ran, can we go on the Big Dipper?"

I'm squinting up at the blue sky, watching the bright-patterned car creep over the top of the scaffolding mountain. It pours itself down the rickety cliff with its cargo screaming.

"Do you really want to?"

Perhaps she hates the idea. But, then, she is a bit old, I suppose.

"It's OK if you'd rather not," I tell her.

She smiles at me. She's wearing her floppy straw hat with the unravelling brim. "Come on, then," she says.

We set off through the crowds.

There's a queue waiting for the Big Dipper. It stretches right past the Hall of Mirrors to the slot machines behind the Dodgem cars. We'll be standing here for ages.

"One-arm bandits!" says Gran, spotting the machines. "Splendid. We can gamble while we wait." She's fishing in the pocket of her crumpled linen coat and gives me a coin. It'll be no good, of course, but I push it in the slot.

Lemons and bells and all the other things fly past in the row of windows then stop with a click. Zilch.

Gran's machine is spinning as well. It gives a bad-tempered clank, and coins start pouring out of it, an absolute torrent of them, cascading into its trough and spilling over onto the wooden planks of the pier's deck.

"Bingo!" she says, gathering up the richness. "Help yourself."

People are staring enviously, it's quite embarrassing. I try to give my handful of money to Gran to drop in her pockets with the rest, but she laughs and says, "Don't be silly. It's just for fun, isn't it? Easy come, easy go."

I wonder if my machine could win, as well.

I'm interested in it now, though I wasn't before. I push a coin in its slot and the pictures spin, but it still does nothing.

"That's how they make their profits," Gran says. "People want to win more, so they put all the cash back in again. But we didn't have to earn it, did we? So play again if you want to. It's just a game."

A game.

Someone else was talking about a game. I can't think who it was.

"We've lost our place in the queue," I say.

People moved past while we were grovelling about among our winnings.

"Doesn't matter," says Gran. "The sun's shining and we've all this treasure to spend. Tell you what – go and get a couple of ice creams. I'll stay here and keep our place. Here – have some more money."

"Gran, don't be daft, I've got masses. What flavour d'you want?"

"Chocolate and pink," she says. "One of those twin cones."

She's nearly up to the Big Dipper pay-desk by

the time I come back – there was a queue at the ice-cream stall.

"Lovely," she says. "Thank you very much."

"Gran –" I lick a raspberry dribble off my knuckles – "Did they have ice creams when you were a girl?"

"Oh, yes. We loved the ice-cream man. He rode a tricycle with a cold box on it, and rang a bell. *Stop Me and Buy One.*"

"Is that what he said?"

"It was written on the tricycle's fridge. Big blue letters. I loved it when he lifted the lid. Cold mist came out and it was all frosty inside, so the ices creaked when you moved them. He had cones and choc-ices, or you could have a slab between wafers. A sandwich, it was called."

"And ice lollies?"

Gran takes another lick and shakes her head. "Things on sticks hadn't been invented. We had water ices, though – triangular bars that you ate out of their wrappers. Checked blue and white, they were. I loved the colours. Lemon, orange, pink, lime-green. Then the war came, and ices disappeared."

"Why?"

"I never knew, really. We were short of everything. No luxuries, nothing nice. It was very boring."

"*Boring?*" I knew war was dangerous, but I never thought it was boring.

"The boredom was the worst thing, actually."

"Worse than guns and bombs?"

"No. But the war only got really bad occasionally."

She's got ice cream on her nose. She wipes it off on the back of her hand.

"Two little girls in our road were killed," she says. "That was sad."

"Weren't you scared?"

"Not really. I worried about my dad when there was a bad raid and he was on fire-watch duty in the city, but I never thought the war could hurt me. I felt very fierce. And excited, of course. Danger is very exciting."

Another carload of screaming people drops like a snake over the top of the Dipper. Yes, Gran's right. That's why we're all waiting here, to scream in terror. My knees feel funny at the thought of it, as if I want to run very fast, but I have to stand still and wait my turn to be scared. And it's not dangerous really, or it wouldn't be allowed. It's just pretend. The real thing might be different.

"I wish I knew what war's like."

"I hope you never do," Gran says. She's not smiling.

I can see her point. It must have been awful that the little girls got killed. But she knows about something I can't even imagine, and I kind of envy her that.

It's dark. We're going across the garden, and I'm shivering in my dressing gown. The frosty grass is crunching under my slippers.

"Quickly," Mum says.

Her torch doesn't show much, just the bit of white grass in front of us. There's a slotted cowl on it that only lets the light out in narrow strips so it can't be seen from an aeroplane. You're not allowed to use a torch without a cowl.

We've come to the path. The paving stones are slippery with frost. In the summer, there are ants under them, and on hot days they swarm and the new ones with wings go flying off. I suppose they're asleep now.

"Put that light out!" a man shouts from the road.

"We're just going to the shelter," Mum shouts back.

"Doesn't matter, put it out."

Mum switches the torch off. We can see the long beams of searchlights swinging to and fro across the sky, looking for the raiding planes. There's a crackle of orange tracer fire from distant guns.

We grope our way down the wooden steps to the shelter. There's a thick blanket hung at the door and Mum holds it aside so I can squeeze in ahead of her. The place smells oily because of the hurricane lamp hanging from its nail in the wall. The Marshes are already there, sitting on the bunks, drinking beer. They're our next door neighbours, and the shelter is between our two gardens. Their dog is snoring on the floor. His name's Trevor. I quite like him, but he's smelly. Beer, oil and dog, that's what the shelter smells of. And earth, and damp concrete.

I climb into the top bunk and pull the blanket over me. I keep my dressing gown on. I'm supposed to go back to sleep, but my feet are freezing. I wish I was back in my warm bed in the house, but it's too dangerous when there's a raid on.

The drone of planes is louder and closer. The anti-aircraft guns open up suddenly with deafening bangs.

The curtain is lifted aside and a man in a steel helmet looks in. "You all right in here?" It's the Air-Raid Warden who shouted at us from the street.

"Fine," says Mum. "You coming in?"

"Just for a minute."

He looks very big in his uniform greatcoat. He sits down on the edge of a bunk.

"Like a beer, Phil?" Mr Marsh asks him.

"No, thanks, I'm on duty."

He gropes in his pocket for a handkerchief and blows his nose, which has started to run because it's warmer in here than outside. He tilts his tin hat back and takes his glasses off to wipe his eyes. They're funny eyes, a pale, whitish blue, like a codfish.

"Just be careful of that torch, won't you," he says to my mother.

"I will," she promises.

I don't know why she doesn't tell him he's being stupid. You're allowed to use a torch as long as it has a cowl on it, and ours has. I pick it up to show him, but he's settling his glasses on his nose again and doesn't notice. Mum's looking at him with a brave little smile, as if she's willing to do whatever he says. I don't like the Warden.

There are heavier thuds from outside now, a series of them, getting closer. They shake the earth.

Trevor has raised his head from the folded blanket he lies on. He gets to his feet and puts his chin on Mrs Marsh's lap, and she strokes his head. "There, pet, it's all right." He wags his tail a bit, but he doesn't lie down.

A whistling sound starts screaming down towards us.

"Whoops," says Mr Marsh.

There's an enormous bang. Another whistle is building up, even louder—

The crash is deafening. The shelter's walls seem to do an in-out puff like a bellows, and the Hurricane lamp bucks on the wall. My eyes are shut and my arms are clutched over my head.

74

The third explosion is on the other side of us, a bit further away.

"Straddled," I hear Mr Marsh say. "Lucky."

The concrete ceiling might have come in on us, and we'd have been crushed under broken concrete and tons of earth. That happened to some people in Lewisham, Mum told me. But it hasn't happened here. We're all right.

"Better go and have a look," the Warden says. He turns to lift the curtain aside. A smell of dust and smoke and earth drifts in. There's a shifting red light of fire and people are shouting urgently.

Mum puts her hand on the sleeve of his uniform greatcoat. "Do be careful."

He looks back at her and says, "Don't worry."

He goes out.

The curtain falls back into place.

The Big Dipper is scarier than I thought. Gran and I got in the first car, like the front seat on the top of a bus, only no windows to look through – nothing. We chugged up the first climb – and at the top the car tipped forward and dropped down like a stone, SCREAM, SCREAM, going to fall out, down, down, down. Now the track's rising like a wall in front of us – over the top, round a bend, down and down again, SCREAM.

Gran's not screaming, I don't think she can. She's clutching the bar in front of us with one hand, and the other one's clamped on her straw hat. Its edges are flapping wildly. It's going to blow away. She looks terrified.

"Take your hat off!" I shout. "Hold it on your lap!"

"*What?*" She can't hear in the screaming and rattling.

I shout it louder.

"*I can't!*" she yells in my ear. "*My brain will fall out.*"

Mad old bat, I do love her.

The afternoon is still warm, but there's shadow over Gran's steep garden with its trickling fountain among the ferns. We're sitting out here with tea and cherry cake. I'm lying back in my deckchair, looking at the leaves against the still-bright sky. I'm chasing something in my mind that I can't quite remember.

"Mum wasn't alive in the war, was she?"

Gran laughs. "No, love, she wasn't even thought of. I was only a kid myself." After a minute she adds, "Why do you ask?"

"I thought she was in an air-raid shelter. It must have been a dream."

"I love dreaming," says Gran.

"Do you?"

"Oh, yes. I look forward to it all day – being warm and cosy in bed with a good book, waiting for a dream to start."

"Don't you go to sleep first and dream afterwards?"

"Only if I'm very tired." She laughs. "Then I wake at three in the morning with the light still on and my glasses squashed sideways. Dreaming first is much better."

"How do you do that?" I really want to know.

She thinks for a moment. "You have to let your brain go kind of soft. Stop it working. If it goes all reasonable and starts observing things, like, *This is me, trying to have a dream,* then you've had it. Nobody can dream on purpose, you just have to let it happen."

She seems to know a lot about it.

"Gran?"

"Yes, love?"

"When you're in a dream, do you *know* you're dreaming?"

"Not really," she says. "If I start to suspect I'm dreaming, I'll think I've woken up, but I haven't – it's just shifted to something else. All dreams are real while they're happening – you only know they weren't real when you actually *do* wake up."

I'm nodding slowly – at least, I think I am, but I might be dreaming at this very moment. There's no way I can tell.

I want to find out. I shut my eyes, trying hard to test the truth of what's all round me. The canvas of the deckchair is firm, it bears my weight, but I'm pushing against it, trying to move, checking that I can sit up, lean forward, get to my feet.

There's something wrong. I'm too heavy, I'm not strong enough, the simple effort I'm making is hurting me—

"That's a good girl. Gently now, we're just moving you a little bit—"

"She won't hear you."

It hurts, it hurts.

I want to scream but I can't.

There's a sound like a little squeak of terror.

It might be me.

"Touch and go," someone else says. "All we can do is pray."

We're in some enormous church with tall pillars that fan out at the top to make an intricate ceiling. It's so shadowed, I can hardly see the details, it's like the network of branches in a dark forest.

Nice, fat Cara has lit a candle. She's reaching forward to put it in a stand with dozens of others, some of them white and new, others guttering their last in a puddle of melted wax. She stands back and links her hands, bowing her head. Now she makes the sign of the cross.

"Tig, don't you want to light a candle?" she asks.

I shake my head. I don't feel right in here. Mum and I have never been to church. When I was in primary school the girl next door tried to get me to go to Sunday school, and when I asked Mum she said, "By all means, if you'd like to." But she didn't look at me, just kept her eyes on the book she was reading, and I thought I'd better not.

"It's for Ken," Cara reminds me. "Poppy's older brother. He's in the Army, in North Africa, she had a letter yesterday. Don't you want to say a prayer for him, keep him safe?"

She doesn't have to remind me who Ken is. But she doesn't know about that evening when he saw me home, and kissed me. Nobody knows.

Cara's watching me. "Just to show you care," she says.

I give in. I take a candle and offer its tip to the flame of a burning one. After a moment, the wick catches and my candle has its own flame. I wedge it carefully in the runny wax of an empty holder, and make sure it's standing straight.

Ken. Will I ever see you again?

It's not much of a question to God, if there is a God, and I know the answer anyway. Ken has moved on. It was only a kiss, and he is a soldier now. He will not remember.

But I want to see him again.

Cara puts a coin in the wooden box, paying for my prayer.

*   *   *

There's a seagull on the roof, pale grey and white, with a curved yellow beak. The sky behind it is still blue and cloudless though it's evening now and Gran's garden is cool. The tea things have gone, and there's a smell of frying onions from the kitchen.

The tiredness is falling away. In a minute, I'll fold up the deckchairs and put them in the shed by the end wall.

Not quite yet. I need to go on looking at the seagull.

This is real, isn't it?

Please let this be real.

The kitchen smells of soapy washing. This is Monday, but it rained all day, so the clothes are hanging to dry in here. They make it seem shadowed and damp, but it's too cold to do homework in my room upstairs. Mum's lit a fire in the front room, but I'm not going in there, not while she's talking to the Air Raid Warden.

He's been dropping in ever since the night when the house across the road got bombed. He's always got some excuse, like he's inspecting the blackout curtains or checking the sandbags. I don't see how you can check a sandbag, it's either on the front doorstep like it's supposed to be, or it isn't. He says the bags rot when they get wet, but we know that.

Tonight he brought four eggs. He and his wife keep hens.

His wife never comes to see Mum, just him, in the evenings when he's on duty. At school today Kate asked if he was my mum's boyfriend. I told her not to be so stupid. Everyone giggled then looked at the ceiling and pretended they weren't.

I hate the girls at school. Well, most of them. Meg's all right, and Poppy and Cara. Kate, too, of course. But I hate the ones who belong to the tennis club and go to parties and talk about boys all the time. They raise their eyebrows if I say anything, and glance at each other and laugh. I shouldn't have told them I'm a Communist, they've been snotty ever since.

I don't care. Ken understood.

It's dark. I'm not often out after dark because of the raids, but things have been quiet for a bit, so Mum doesn't mind. I'm walking beside Ken, and my hand is in his.

"It was a good meeting," he says.

We've come from Meg's house. The Young Communist League meets there. Her Dad's in the fire brigade – he's secretary of their union.

I wish I could think what to say to Ken. I love the way his black hair flops over his forehead. There's a blue scar across his nose, just a faint blue line. Poppy says it's because he fell out of a tree when he was small, and smashed his face in. I suppose she should know, being his sister.

We're nearly at my house. He'll be going on up the road to the bus stop.

"We've got to get the vote at eighteen," he's saying. "Having to wait until you're twenty-one is ridiculous."

"You get called up for the army at seventeen and a half," I agree, "so you're old enough to fight and maybe get killed, but not to vote. Crazy, isn't it?"

He glances at me and says, "You ought to go into politics, you know."

I laugh.

"No, seriously," he goes on. "They'll need people like us when the war's over. Strong people, with new ideas."

"Do you think so? Really?" How weird, to be

called a strong person. How marvellous.

"Of course they will. We can't go back to the same old mess, millions out of work, slum housing, kids with rickets. We've got to start again."

He'll be leaving school in a few weeks. He's going to Oxford to study politics and economics, but he'll have to do his two years in the army first.

I hate being a schoolgirl. I'm not a child any more but I don't count as a grown-up. I'm nothing. I wish Mum had let me leave when I was fourteen. I could have got a job at the garage on the corner where they make machine guns, though nobody's supposed to know in case of spies. At least I could have said I'm a worker.

We've reached my house. There's a tarpaulin over the roof because the bomb across the road blew half the tiles off. The front garden's a mess of trampled mud. The fence has gone, and the windows are still boarded up. We'll get new glass when the repair squad gets round to it, but they've a lot to do.

We stop where the gate used to be.

"I live here," I tell him.

Ken turns to look at me. "You'll go to university, won't you?" he says. "Next year?"

"Maybe."

It seems unlikely. I'm not one of the clever ones who remember everything. I only like art and English. And French, as long as it's not Racine – all those cedillas and seventeenth century spelling.

"You must," Ken says. "It's a waste if you don't."

"You're joking," I say.

"No, I'm not."

He puts his arms round me. Being so close to him is wonderful.

No one's ever kissed me except Mum, and her kiss is light and quick. This is different, a long, warm pressure on my mouth. For a moment I'm startled and almost pull away – but now I want it to go on for ever.

He's releasing me. He's stepped back.

"Good night, Tig," he says. "And good luck."

He touches my sleeve lightly, then turns away and walks on up the road.

* * *

The Warden is leaving, thank goodness. About time, too.

"Goodnight, Joy," I hear him say. "Thanks for the tea."

"Thank you for the eggs," she says. "That was really kind of you. Goodnight, Phil."

The front door closes, so I gather up my books and go into the sitting room. The fire is burning brightly, Mum's been reckless about piling on the coal.

"Why did you hide away in the kitchen?" She sounds annoyed. "It's really rather rude. Very unwelcoming."

She puts their two empty coffee cups on a tray with a milk jug and sugar bowl. We don't use a milk jug when we're alone, it's all right from the bottle. And neither of us takes sugar.

"I can't do homework with people talking."

"You do it with the radio on."

"That's different."

She tightens her lips and picks up the tray. I open the door to let her go through, but she doesn't say thank you.

I can hear the tap turned on in the kitchen. She's washing the cups. There's the squeak of the pulley wheels as she lets the airer down. She's going to do the ironing. I ought to help. She did the washing this morning before I was up, and she's been working at the library all day. Got to pay the rent, as she says. But it's not my fault the school sets all this homework.

"You're doing very well," Jacoby remarks.

The seagull flies up from the chimney and is lost among the others that wheel and scream over the roof of Gran's house. The garden has turned cool. I rub my arms. I must go upstairs and get my fleece.

"Where have you been?" I ask. It seems a long time since I saw him.

"Around," he says. "Are you enjoying the game?"

"Not much."

"Why not?"

"I was in this poky house, having an argument with Mum. You call that fun?"

I can still see that miserable kitchen with green paint on the walls.

"That's what I mean about doing well," Jacoby says. "You're starting to get the hang of it. You know where you've been."

"So what's good about that? Just look at the place."

There are ebony elephants on the mantelpiece, and the hearthrug has a brown scorch mark because someone let the hot poker roll off the fireplace. It could have been me, I suppose. The fire has burned low now – my arms are chilly.

"You see?" says Jacoby. "You say *Look at it*, and we're looking. Like I say, your skills are improving."

He's sitting beside me on this uncomfortable settee. It's made of slippery stuff like brown leather, only it isn't leather, there are patches of pale canvas showing through where the brown stuff has worn off.

I don't know what he means about improving.

"I get terrible marks for French. And I've all this Racine to translate."

Jacoby's eyes narrow a little.

"You're forgetting," he says. "You don't have to be here, bothering your head about French homework. You're free to move around, aren't you? That's what the game is about."

* * *

I've hauled my pink fleece out of my bag because my arms were cold – but I don't need it. This little bedroom at the top of Gran's house still holds the heat of the day. I can see the yellow sun, low behind the treetops. I sit down on the bed with the fleece beside me, and Jacoby starts kneading it with his front paws, shifting his weight from side to side.

There's something I have to ask him.

"Jacoby?"

"Mmm?"

"If I found somewhere really nice, through playing this go-back game—"

"Yes?"

"And if I liked it so much that I wanted to stay there – would it mean I couldn't go anywhere else? Would I have to leave all this behind?"

He looks up from his kneading. "All what?"

"This house. The garden. The sun and the trees and everything."

"No problem," Jacoby says. "It's with you."

"Oh, good."

Gran's playing the piano downstairs. It's something by Chopin, very sad and beautiful.

"And Gran," I add. "And Mum. Could they come, too?"

I get cross with Mum, but only because she never seems to know I love her.

"Of course."

"Really?"

I'm so pleased, I could hug him.

"You're connected, you see," he goes on. "When you truly love someone, it's like an invisible spider thread that joins you."

"Even in the game?"

"Specially in the game. That's what makes it work. Actually," he adds, "that's *all* that makes it work."

A spider thread.

What if it should break? I stare at Jacoby, and danger seems to surround us. I feel he may vanish if I don't hold him here through looking at him. There's something dreadful at the back of my mind. Suddenly I'm breathless and shaky.

He looks up. "Tell me," he says.

The piece Gran is playing comes to an end, and the room is very quiet.

I'm trying to find words I can bear to say.

"What if someone – goes away? Not just to

another house or something. I mean, for ever?"

He's unruffled. "You mean, if they die."

I gather him up, and his blackness enfolds me.

He doesn't try to free himself, though he's never liked being held for too long. After a bit I let him go, and he settles on the fleece again.

He gives his fur a brief lick then says, "You're bound to find dying a puzzle. It's better when you know how it works."

"But dying *doesn't* work," I object. "That's the whole point. It's the end. That's why it's so scary."

"It's not the total end," he says. "It's just the end of being connected to that particular system. It happened to me, as you may remember."

I can't quite remember, but I know there was a terrible pain.

"It's horrid for people who loved you," he agrees. "One of your spider threads has broken, and it hurts just like breaking a bone."

"Yes."

"Bones can heal and they work fine again, but a broken thread doesn't mend. As far as you are concerned, the person you loved has left your world. It hurts every time you think about it."

"Yes," I say again.

He's going to tell me he's not really here. My hands are covering my face, I don't want to know.

Jacoby puts a paw on my knee. "Keep listening," he says. "It's going to get better now."

I shake my head. It can't get better.

"Yes, it *can*," he insists. "The point is, once you leave what people call the real life, you belong in all times. You can move around as you wish. That's the way I am - and you are, too. At the moment."

Gran has begun to play another piece downstairs. It's happening at the moment.

I am stroking Jacoby *at the moment*. I can feel the strength of his body under his black fur. I can see the dark shape of him against the pink fleece that's pressed down by his weight. Can I be in other moments as well as this one?

"Don't ask," he says gently. "Just enjoy them as they happen."

Enjoy them …

What does he mean?

I've forgotten what we were talking about.
I go on stroking his soft fur.
Perhaps I'm lost.
Perhaps it doesn't matter.

Kate and I are grabbing our lunch break in Oxford Street. It's nearly three o'clock, but this is the week before Christmas, and we've been frantic in the shop. I didn't think we were going to get a break at all, but Mrs Marsh took pity on us.

We're at the coffee stall round the corner, warming our hands on steaming mugs of tea – it's a penny cheaper than coffee. The man who runs it doesn't mind us bringing our own sandwiches. I've got my coat on over my black dress, but it's freezing cold out here. Still, it makes a change from the stuffy air of the Lingerie Department.

A woman walks past with her hand tucked through a man's arm. She looks wonderful. She's wearing grey suede shoes with little heels and narrow straps, and the fur collar of her coat is turned up to frame her face. Her blonde hair is permed into ridges and her lips are painted into a thin red bow. She's smiling. So she should. She and her husband – or whoever he is – are carting loads of bags and parcels, Christmas wrapped.

"Lucky thing," says Kate.

I laugh. There's no point in envying the lucky ones, you'd drive yourself mad that way.

"No, honestly," Kate goes on. "People that rich make me sick. The way they swan into the shop and expect instant service, never mind if there's others waiting."

I agree about that. "It's the ones who turn nasty I can't stand. You daren't ask them to hang on for a moment, or they get you sacked for rudeness."

"Too right. Look at poor Sally Richardson."

"That was awful. She had to tell this enormous woman we didn't have a corset her size—"

"—and lost her job for being cheeky." Kate sighs, envious again. "All the same, just fancy being able to walk into somewhere like our shop and buy whatever you want. Silk stockings, jewellery, evening dresses, perfume – it's not fair."

Mum would never let me say that. *What makes you think life is fair?* she'd ask.

But Kate won't like that, so I tell her, "Things will be different when the war starts. The men will be in the forces, so women will have to do all sorts of work. They'll think twice about sacking us then."

Kate's not convinced. "My dad says there won't be a war. He was in the last one, '14–18. He says the government won't let it happen again."

I haven't got a dad, but Mum's new friend seems to know a lot about everything. She's always quoting him.

"Philip says we have to go to war, otherwise Germany will invade. And they're *fascists*, they'll make life dreadful for everyone."

"That's what they told us last time. Dad was a foreman in a factory, but he thought he ought to join up. He was in the trenches in France and got wounded and gassed, and, when he came back, his firm didn't want him any more. A woman was doing his job, for less money."

"I can see how he felt. But he's working now, isn't he?"

"He's a clerk in an office. Pen-pushing, he calls it. He thinks it's a comedown – and the money's rubbish. Thirty bob a week."

"He'll be glad you've got a job then."

"*Glad?*" says Kate. "You must be joking. He hates me going out to work, he says it's a man's right and duty to support his family. But I couldn't sit around at home, having to ask him for every little thing." She drains her tea mug. "Come on, we must go."

There's a crowd blocking the street by the traffic lights. There were a lot of people when we came out, but there are far more now, filling up both pavements. They're unemployed men. Thin faces, shabby clothes. Some of them are clutching armfuls of posters.

"'Scuse me," Kate says as she pushes her way between them. "Got to get back to work."

98

It's a bit tactless, I suppose.

A man says, "Aren't you the lucky one. All right for some."

He's holding a placard that says in big, red letters, *National Unemployed Workers' Movement.* WORK OR BREAD.

He goes to the edge of the pavement and shouts through a megaphone, "Ready, lads! On the next red light. All together."

The traffic lights turn from green to amber then red, and the traffic come to a halt. The men walk into the road, eight abreast, in step like soldiers. Most of them *are* ex-soldiers, I expect. Kate and I stop to watch.

"They're lying down!" says Kate.

The road is filling with a solid blanket of men lying head to toe and side by side, close-packed and motionless. The organizers are stooping among them, covering them with WORK OR BREAD posters. I think of the war and shiver. It's as though these were corpses being covered with makeshift shrouds. The pattern of red and black letters fills the road completely, a human carpet where cabs and buses and vans were thundering past a moment ago.

A steady chant rises from the hidden men.

"We want work or bread."

It sounds like a choir of ghosts.

The lights have turned to green. Engines rev up. People watching from the pavement scream in horror, thinking the living carpet is going to be run over – I'm screaming, too.

It's all right. Not a car or a bus has moved.

There's a pause, and the lights change back to red.

A policeman is blowing his whistle. He shouts, "Get up, you fellows, you're blocking the traffic."

Everyone laughs at him, and the men don't move.

A woman beside me says, "What are they supposed to live on, poor souls? They've got nothing."

More police are arriving. Two of them grab a man and drag him away by his arms. He doesn't resist. His feet trail on the ground. Another unemployed man steps into his place and lies down. Horns are hooting. The blocked traffic stretches right back along Oxford Street.

The police go on hauling men away, but it's

like trying to dam a floodtide. As soon as a gap in the carpet is made, another body fills it.

A sweating policeman appeals to the crowd. "Can we have some help here, please?"

Nobody steps forward. Nobody even meets his eye.

Kate's turned away. "Come *on*," she says over her shoulder. "We'll be late."

She pushes through the crowd, with me close behind her.

As soon as there's enough space, we run.

"You know what they're going to do next, don't you?" says Mum.

We're in our little flat over the chemist's shop. Tea is on the table.

"The unemployed, you mean? No, I don't know."

"A big crowd of them are going to walk into the Ritz and ask for tea. Probably a hundred or more."

"The *Ritz*?" I can't believe it. "Unemployed men in the *Ritz*?"

That grand hotel is so posh, you'd think it owns the pavement as well. I was walking past it last week and nearly got knocked flat by their doorman. He barged forward in his gold-braided uniform and top hat to whistle for a taxi, flung up his white-gloved hand – and hit me a smack on the shoulder. Never apologized. It was like he didn't see I was there. Or he thought I shouldn't be.

"The actual Ritz," Mum confirms.

"But – tea in there must cost a week's wages. More, perhaps. And the unemployed don't have any wages."

"That's the point. They won't get served, obviously – they'll be thrown out. They know that. But it'll be quite a sight, all these unemployed ex-soldiers being ejected into the street. The press will be there to take photos."

She fills my cup.

"How do you know the press will be there?" I ask.

"Philip told me. He knows one of the organizers. He met him at the Evening Institute."

"Oh. Right."

"You ought to enrol at the Institute," Mum says. "Get some better education. You don't want to be selling female underwear for the rest of your life, do you?"

I don't know what I want. There's no point in wondering. I just do what I can do.

"Look at Philip," she goes on. "When he was fourteen, his father died."

I've heard this before, but she's going to tell me again.

"He'd hoped to go to university, but there were three younger ones, and his mother couldn't cope. So Phil had to leave school and work in an iron foundry."

I don't feel particularly sympathetic. People have worse things happen to them.

"He wanted to be a lawyer," Mum goes on. "But he hasn't given up. He's aiming at a scholarship to Ruskin College. Oxford," she adds, in case I'm not properly impressed.

"I don't want to be a lawyer."

"No, but you can be *something*."

I shrug. There's no way I can measure up to the wondrous Saint Philip.

"Actually," Mum says after a pause, "I thought I might ask him round after work on Friday. For high tea. He'd love to meet you."

How I can manage to be out?

No, I mustn't be uncharitable. Philip may be quite human, for all I know. It's just I'm sick of getting him rammed down my neck.

"Fine," I say. But the pause I left has done its damage.

Mum's pushed her plate away, the pilchard on toast half-eaten. She's leaning her head on her hand, stirring her tea.

Sorry, Mum. Sorry.

I ought to say it aloud, but I can't. That's stupid, isn't it. Why shouldn't she have a boyfriend if she wants one? I'm not a child any more, I'm fourteen, I can manage, I'm working.

But—

He'll come to live here, I know he will.

Mum and I will never be able to talk to each other without him hearing.

He might see me in my knickers.

He'll start telling me what to do.

I'll have to leave home.

I don't earn enough to rent a room of my own, so I'll have to get married, and I don't want to get married, not yet, perhaps not ever.

"I'd love to be a divorced woman," says Poppy.

"So *wicked.*"

Her voice comes from above me. We're perched in our favourite oak tree on the Common. She's got the best place today – there's a sort of natural seat where the trunk divides into two main limbs. I'm on the branch below, with my back to the trunk. We take turns.

"I mean," Poppy goes on, "just fancy the *King of England* being in love with you."

She's talking about Mrs Simpson, of course. The whole country is talking about Mrs Simpson, the outrageous woman who got a divorce from Mr Simpson, whoever he may be. They say King Edward is going to give up the throne so he can marry her.

"I don't see why he can't marry her and keep on being king," I say.

Poppy laughs. "You're as bad as Ken," she says. "He thinks the king is wonderful, of course."

Ken is Poppy's older brother. He's very clever. I wouldn't tell her, but it gives me a kind of thrill, looking at him. He's got this dark hair that flops over his eyebrows. He fell off his bike when he was six, Poppy says, and it left this blue mark across his nose. And he's a Communist. But—

"I'm surprised Ken likes any kind of king."

"He doesn't usually," Poppy agrees. "King Edward's different, though. When he went to South Wales, he insisted on seeing where the miners lived. He said it was disgraceful, they ought to have decent houses."

"So they should."

"Well, yes. But all these important people had to wait for hours while the king poked around in miners' cottages."

"Brilliant," I say.

"But anyway –" Poppy sounds decided – "I want to be like Mrs Simpson. Rich and divorced and fascinating."

"I don't know that she's rich."

"She will be if she marries the king."

I'm not convinced.

"My mum says being a divorced woman is really tough." Or maybe Mum means any woman who's on her own.

"Why?"

"She never gets invited anywhere, because

106

she hasn't got a partner."

"Can't she go on her own?"

"Hostesses are scared she'd steal their husbands."

Poppy gives a snort of amusement and says, "Honestly, this country is so stuffy. How can one be Bohemian? I'll have to go to Paris, that's all. Or Vienna."

"What's Bohemian?"

"Oh, you know. Being unconventional and arty. Dripping around in Japanese kimonos. Smoking cigarettes through long holders. Drinking that green stuff – what's it called?"

"Absinthe."

I know about absinthe, because of the art books Mum brings home from the library.

"It's like gin only more so," I tell her. "It drives you mad. There was a French painter who used to drink it, and he died. Toulouse-Lautrec or somebody."

"I knew you'd know," says Poppy. After a pause, she adds, "Vienna's no good, actually, I can't speak German. I'll have to stick with Paris." She leans out from her perch to look down at me. "You're good at French. Why don't we go together?"

"Why not?" I say lazily. "We'll be dancers."

I'm still thinking of the art book. Fish-net stockings, a froth of petticoats, a velvet band round the throat.

But this is Poppy's dream, not mine. It's very nice, but it isn't the sort that comes true.

"You're going back very nicely," Jacoby remarks.

We're walking across the Common, kicking through rustling heaps of brown leaves.

"Am I?"

Like an idiot, I look down. The toes of my feet are coming out in turn from below the hem of my skirt, taking me forward in the usual way.

"Back in time," he says patiently. "You've reached 1936. The abdication year."

"What's abdication?"

"When a king or queen gives up the throne."

A flash of memory comes.

"You mean King Edward really did it? Married Mrs Simpson and stopped being king?"

"He did indeed."

"What happened afterwards? Did they have to leave the country?"

"Yes, the very next day."

"Who was king after that?"

"Edward's younger brother, George. He ruled all the way through the war. Why are we talking about kings?"

"Why not?"

"Oh, all right. I suppose you like them. After all, we're looking for something you'll like."

We walk on. He runs off to do a bit of leaf-chasing, then comes back.

"How about the shop?" he enquires. "I thought you might enjoy that. You seemed keen on shopping."

I remember that, too. It seems easy when Jacoby's around. I laugh.

"Ten hours a day for eight-and-six a week, and you thought I'd enjoy it? You must be joking. Couldn't you have made up something better?"

He stares at me, appalled.

"I don't make the game *up*!" he says.

"Oh. I thought you did."

"Of course not. I'm – what shall we say? – your tour guide. But the places we go to are real. The things that happen to you *have happened* to somebody. They are history."

There's something quite wrong about that.

"But Jacoby, there are things nobody else would know. Stuff about me and Gran and Mum. Personal stuff."

"It's personal to you. But it doesn't stop being history just because nobody else knows."

"I wasn't alive in 1936. Neither was Mum. I'm not even sure that Gran was."

Jacoby sighs as if I'm being silly. "I've told you before," he says, "once you've left the system people call Here and Now, you can be anywhere and anywhen. Going back doesn't stop just because you pass a date that mattered in the other life. You could say, if you like, that you're dreaming in history. Do you see?"

"I think so." I'm not sure, but I suppose I have to take his word for it.

"Good."

We walk on through the brown leaves. The red sun is low behind the trunks of the bare trees. It's getting cold.

The fire is almost out. I pick up the tongs and put a couple of small lumps of coal on, but it's not going to catch without some sticks.

I go through the kitchen to the coal shed outside, picking up the torch from the dresser. It's raining.

Mum must have forgotten to get firewood. There's nothing but an old vegetable crate, half-demolished. I stamp on it to break some more bits off – mustn't take too much or we'll have no kindling for tomorrow.

Back at the fire, I gently add the sticks, blow at the small glow, feed it with my breath. It's a weak kitten of a thing, but it's just about alive.

I have to darn a hole under the arm of my black dress for the shop, but my fingers are too cold to hold a needle.

My mother is out with Philip.

I don't like this house.

I don't want to be here.

Gran is dusting her grand piano. I'm running the carpet sweeper over the floor, to make the room respectable for her pupils, even though the last one's just gone, and there isn't another until this afternoon. The piano is so black and glossy, it shows a film of dust after just an hour or two.

"There was another car accident this morning," Gran says, "at the crossroads by the church. Bella Whittle saw it on her way here. She was so shaken up, her arpeggios were rubbish, poor child. At least, that was her excuse."

I laugh. But it's bad about the accidents. There really are rather a lot.

"They need notices to say which is the main road," I say. "The way it is now, nobody knows they should stop, so they keep running into each other. It's ridiculous."

"We should have stuck to horses."

Gran dusts her way up the keyboard from the bottom notes to the top, ker-plink, ker-plink, ker-plink, then closes the lid.

"You know where you are with a horse," she goes on. "Mind you, there were some dreadful accidents in London, with silly young men driving spirited thoroughbreds much too fast. But these cars. They've got no sense."

"My friend Cara says there's going to be a driving test," I tell her. "People will have to pass it before they can drive on their own."

"Right and proper, too." Gran plumps up a final cushion. "That'll do," she says, and glances at the clock on the mantelpiece. "Time for coffee. Or shall we be morbid and go down to the crossroads? Just in case there's anything truly dreadful to look at."

We look at each other without allowing a smile, then we both say together, "Let's."

We're by the front door with its panels of blue stained glass, taking our coats from the hallstand. My hand pauses for a moment.

Gran says, "If you think it might be too nasty, we won't go."

I'm shaking my head. I mustn't duck out of doing things just because they might be nasty. I'm pushing my hands into my coat sleeves.

I give a little gasp. Perhaps I turned awkwardly or something.

"There's a good girl. We're just turning you over. Upsy-daisy."

Aaaah.

"Sorry, pet, hang on, we've nearly ..."

"That's the way, all done now."

"Good girl, good girl, better in a minute, this will help ..."

The voices are going further off.
Perhaps I can open my eyes.
No.
Too heavy.
Too difficult.

I'm in a car. It's a big, open car, and it's full of children. I'm squashed in beside Cara. Cara the car girl. She has a smaller brother on her lap. Her mother is in the front with the baby, and her dad is driving.

He's not very good at driving, I don't think he's done it before. The car doesn't belong to him, he's borrowed it for the day to go to Brighton. I couldn't believe it when Cara asked me to come, I said it would make too many, but she said it was fine. I think she thinks I'm lonely.

We're following another car, not very close to it. I'm glad about that, because Cara's dad doesn't always manage to brake very quickly, and when he does, the engine usually stops, and he has to get out with the long handle to start it again.

The car in front is coming to a crossroads.

There's a lorry coming from the left. It's not going to stop, neither is the car, oh, God, there's going to be a—

Tyres scream, a horn hoots and goes on hooting, and the sound is mixed up in the grinding smash of metal. We're skidding sideways, we're going up the bank, the car's lurching sideways, it's going to turn over – no, there's a tree—

Bang.

All our heads nod forward then snap back again as if we've agreed with something violently. My neck hurts. I hurt all over.

Bits of branch have fallen on us from the tree. Cara is picking leaves and bark out of her hair. She seems calm, but the smaller children are crying.

Cara's mother is leaning over from the front seat, clutching the baby, who is crying as well. "Are you all right?" she shouts, as loudly as though the banging and crashing is still going on. "Is everyone all right?"

"We're fine," says Cara.

"Thank God," says her mother, and they both make the sign of the cross.

I'm not fine, but I don't like to say so. I think I

115

hit my side against the edge of the car or something. But the pain of it seems to be fading. That's good.

Cara's father has got out of the car. He's joined the crowd round the wreckage in the middle of the crossroads. Someone is screaming in short bursts that sound breathless.

People have come out to stare and tut, standing with folded arms. A woman in an apron pushes her way to the crashed car that's half underneath the lorry and says, "I live across there by the church. We use my house as the dressing station now we get all these accidents. Someone help this lady in. Can you walk, dear?" she adds to the screaming woman in the car.

The woman's husband has got out of the car. "Of *course* she can't," he says. "Look at her. For heaven's sake—" There's blood running down his own face, but he seems unaware of it. "Isn't there a telephone in this village? Surely someone must have a telephone? We've got to get an ambulance."

People are shaking their heads.

"Try the big house," a man suggests. "They've got one."

"They don't let people use it, though," his friend says.

"Don't bother," says the woman in an apron. She turns to the boy standing beside her and says, "Stanley, run and get the doctor, quick as you can."

She starts shepherding people across the road to her cottage. The man with blood on his face stays beside his wife in the wrecked car. The lorry driver is climbing out of his cab. He looks dazed.

Cara's father and some other men are inspecting the damage to our car. I go and look as well. It's not as bad as I expected. The front corner has been shoved in where it hit the tree, but otherwise it looks much as it did before.

Cara's dad says to the men, "If we can just prise the wing away from the tyre it might go."

The men fetch tools – a sledgehammer, a pick-axe, a couple of stout bits of wood and several spades. They start heaving and hammering at the dented wing. The metal groans and clangs.

"That's it clear of the tyre," one of them says after a bit. "See if she'll run."

"Need to get her off this bank," Cara's dad says.

They go round to the front of the car and push, but it doesn't move.

"Let the brake off," says someone.

Cara's dad leans in and does something to a lever, and the men push again. The car instantly runs backwards down the bank into the road, nearly flattening a child.

"Whoa!" they shout, as if at a runaway horse. "Hang on! Stop her there."

They all run to hold the car. "Get in, sir," they say to Cara's dad. "Put the handbrake on."

Once that is done, they look underneath the car, and open the bonnet to stare respectfully at its engine.

"Big, isn't it," one of them says. "What a beauty. All that brass."

"Start her up, sir," another suggests. "See if she goes."

Cara's dad feeds the long handle into the front of the car, stooping down over it. He yanks it up – and the engine roars into life.

Everyone cheers. We all get into the car again. The engine settles to a quiet purr. We are going to Brighton, it's all right.

Why have I woken? The room is still dark, it's too early to get up. I reach for the curtain and pull it back. The night sky is streaked with fierce orange above the rooftops. Another day is starting.

I flop back on my pillows. I don't think I want another day. I'm very tired, although I've slept. These dreams I've been having go on and on, there's never a moment when they let me step outside them and look at what's happening from a normal point of view. I don't know what's normal any more. I'm not even sure if this is Gran's house, though it seems to be. The whole thing is getting me down.

"You'll feel better when you've had some breakfast," Jacoby remarks from the end of my bed. He can be so irritating sometimes.

"Can you really imagine that all I need is *cornflakes*?" I demand. "Well, think again. I can't go on with this. I've had enough."

"Enough of the game?"

"Yes."

I'm glad he's reminded me. That's the whole trouble – his stupid game.

"Why?" he enquires. "What's the matter with it?"

"I want to go back to being real. Like I was before all this started."

He comes plodding up the duvet towards me. He's looking bothered.

"There are technical difficulties," he says.

"What do you mean?"

"Things have changed. They're not what they were before you started. You know that, don't you?"

His yellow glance sends a sudden spasm of pain through me, and I gasp.

It's all right – I'm back here now. Just for a

second, he sent me to a place where everything hurts.

"I didn't send you," he protests. "You wanted to be real, and you were. But it isn't much fun at present, as I keep telling you."

He's right. When I go to that place, I can't move and everything's terrible.

The truth hits me like a cold draught. It's not the place that's changed – it's me.

Dread churns in my stomach. I used to be strong and quick. I could run upstairs, dance, ride a bike. Has all that gone? Is there nothing for me to return to?

"There probably will be," Jacoby says, picking up my thoughts. "You'll have to decide eventually. Meanwhile, you can run and dance in the game. Ride a bike if you want to. I still do a bit of mousing," he adds. "Just to keep my hand in – or paw."

He smiles at something he's remembered.

"I met a very interesting mouse the other day. He'd spent a long time in a cage, running in a wheel. He said he kept wondering what happened to the energy he put into all that running, considering it never got him anywhere. We discussed it for quite a while."

"You're weird, you know. How can you be talking to a mouse one minute and chasing him the next?"

"Different mice," says Jacoby.

I go on thinking about the mouse and his energy. It's almost like the question that's kept nagging at me.

"Something worrying you?" Jacoby enquires.

"Well, yes. It's about the way time works."

"Go on."

I frown, trying to get it clear in my mind.

"If I go back a long way – dreaming in history, like you said – are the years in between now and that earlier time still around?"

"Of course they are."

I'm not sure he sees what I'm asking. Perhaps I need to spell it out better.

"We were walking through a wood, weren't we? And you said I'd been in 1936."

"Yes."

"But I didn't know I'd gone back all those years. It seemed like it was happening now."

"So it was."

"No, Jacoby, listen. Nineteen thirty-six is a

very long time ago. We've had –" I can't do the numbers but I can see them like shapes – "about three quarters of a century since then. But when I was in 1936, I didn't know anything later had happened. It was all in the future."

"Of course it was," Jacoby agrees. "But that doesn't mean it hadn't happened."

I put my hand over my eyes and shake my head.

"It's not possible. You're saying the time between 1936 and where we are now *did actually exist* when I was in 1936?"

"Right."

"And it's just that I didn't know?"

"You couldn't know," he agrees. "You never can."

It doesn't make sense.

I give him a poke with my finger and say, "That's the trouble, don't you see? You're saying the future existed in 1936."

"Yes."

"Well, in that case, the future might exist right now. If I didn't know it was there in 1936, I might not know now."

"Absolutely," says Jacoby. "What's your problem?"

"My problem is, the future *can't* exist. It hasn't happened yet."

"Wrong."

"Huh?"

"All time exists," he says firmly. "You can't see the future, because you're not equipped to, but it's there."

"How do you know?"

"Because of the way I am."

"What way?"

He settles a little closer.

"When you are alive," he explains, "you are joined into time. Like a cogwheel is joined in its machine. You know what cogwheels are?"

"Of course I do. They've got teeth round the edge, so one wheel turns another one. You get them in old clocks, the wind-up sort. But I don't see what you mean about time."

"Time is a turning wheel. Such a huge wheel, you can't see it. That's why people think time goes in a straight line, same as they used to think the earth was flat."

"So how does this wheel work?"

"Everything that lives is turning as well," he says, "right down to the tiniest particles. That's what being alive actually means. Living things are wheels, too. Each one meshes with the wheel of time, like a cog in a gearbox."

I nod slowly. I let the fingertips of one hand roll through the fingertips of the other, like two cogwheels connecting.

"That's right," says Jacoby. "And because you are locked into it, you can't see it from outside. You have memory, of course, so you know what experiences you've had in the wheel system. You're happy with the idea of a past. Everyone knows about the past, they tell each other about it constantly. Look at newspapers, full of stuff about things that have already happened. Look at the Internet. Stacked with what people have done and said and found out. Lots of ideas about the future, right enough – but they're only thought and imagination."

"Of course they are. Nobody can see into the future. We're not equipped, like you said."

"You're not equipped while you're still alive," he corrects.

125

While you're still alive—

I know where this is leading. It's about Jacoby. I take a breath, and manage to say the words steadily.

"You mean, you can see it after you've died."

"Exactly!"

He's beaming at me, pleased that I've understood.

"When you die, you're not locked into time any more," he explains. "You can see the whole thing from outside. You're free to move through all the time there is."

"And how much is there?"

He purrs with amusement at my silly question.

"Nobody can know. It's always been there. It always will be. It goes on for ever."

"But –" I can't get my head round this – "My mum said all things have a beginning and an end."

"That's what everyone says," he agrees. "They see it that way because their own lives have a start and a finish, and they think that's the pattern for everything." He rolls on his back luxuriously, then looks at me again. "Do you know about the Big Bang theory?"

I shake my head.

"It's a suggestion that everything started with a massive cosmic explosion out of nowhere. Such nonsense. There's never been a state of nothing – there never will be. But the Big Bang lot don't get this."

I'm finding it a bit tricky myself.

"It's easy," says Jacoby. "Just relax the mind. Then you can see everything mingles with everything else, on and on. Or back and back, it's the same thing."

"Is it?"

"Of course. Look at the circle a year makes. You go from January to December, and then what happens? You're in January again."

"But that's a new circle."

"Are you sure?"

No, I'm not sure. Then the penny drops, as if into a game machine that's pouring out a shoal of understanding, and I bat my hand against my forehead.

"It's a continuation of the old one," I say. "At midnight on December thirty-first, nothing changes except the number we've given to the year. It's like coiling up a garden hose, circle

127

on circle, but it's all the same hose. Coiled up in layers."

Yes, he's talked about layers.

Jacoby gives me his cat grin, and stretches a long paw towards me. "I knew you'd see it," he says. "I didn't want to mention the hose idea because it's a spiral, and that could have made things more complicated. But yes, you're right. You have a huge advantage, of course," he adds. "At the moment, you're not quite alive. You're a slipping cog. Not absolutely connected."

This is the thing that scares me.

My fingers close for comfort round the smooth, black paw he has extended. I can feel the slender bones under the fur and the sheaths that contain his claws. This is real, isn't it?

No, probably not. I so much wish it was.

Jacoby's paw stretches a little in my hand, and I feel a purr run through him.

"It's very nice to have you here," he says. "Wherever it is."

The rising sun suddenly beams from behind a chimney pot, and the room fills with light.

Light sparkles from the blue pool – the bright

ripples of it dazzle me. I'm sitting on warm, smooth tiles, with my feet in the water and a towel round my shoulders. There's a smell of chlorine and the place is noisy with shouts and laughter and splashing.

It's very grand. There are ornate arches round the pool, with changing rooms beyond them that you can occupy all by yourself if you like – you don't have to share with everyone else. The walls are tiled with marvellously patterned Arabic designs. A bar has been set up at one end, and waiters in white aprons are moving around in a smooth, professional way with trays held one-handed at their shoulders. A jazz band is playing and the music echoes up to the high ceiling where water reflections jump and wriggle. In a long line above the arches, gold mosaic letters say, ST GEORGE'S SWIMMING POOL.

A young man in a striped costume dives into the water, very untidily because he's got a bottle of champagne in one hand. The splash he makes goes all over some girls drinking cocktails on the far side of the pool. They scream and leap up. He waves the bottle above the blue water, shouting, "Come and get it!" They jump in one after the other, splash, splash, splash, they're thrashing around, trying to grab at the bottle, everyone's laughing.

I turn my head to look at the band. The musicians wear white jackets and bow ties. All of them are black. For a moment I wonder if they are white people with their faces made up to kid people they're proper jazz players from New Orleans or somewhere, but, no, these are real Negroes. *I'm glad you've got the job*, I think in a rush of unexpected fellow feeling. *I hope they pay you decently.*

The same feeling makes me look down at my legs and at my feet in the water. For some reason, I expect them to be coffee-brown – but they're not. They're quite pale. This seems surprising, though I don't know why.

Kate said the swimming party was going to be truly scandalous. Perhaps the black jazzmen are what she had in mind. People here think it's deliciously wicked that Negroes should be running their eyes over white girls with nothing on but bathing costumes. They see anyone with a black skin as exotic and dangerous and disgraceful. This is very odd, but I know it's true.

It worries me that I'm not brown. This isn't my real self. I want to apologize to the musicians for looking so different from them.

I wish Mum was here. She might know what's happened.

There she is! It's her, I know it is, walking towards the bar with her hand through the arm of a man in a striped blazer. She's in a white bathing costume with a Japanese kimono over it, patterned with orange chrysanthemums.

She glances at me over her shoulder and says, "Don't be silly, darling, they wouldn't have let you in while you were brown."

"Ridiculous prejudice," says the man. His eyes are the same colour as the pale blue water, but he is wearing white trousers and navy deck shoes under the striped blazer, and doesn't look as if he intends to swim. "Another drink, Joy?"

I'm scrambling up from the pool's edge, I must catch up with her—

There's a cane table with a glass top in the way. Kate and two young men called Bertie and Dibs are sitting beside it on cane chairs.

"Darling!" Kate says, putting up a hand as I

131

almost collide with her. "You're just in time for more drinkies. Look – heavenly Manhattans." She's smoking a cigarette through a long holder.

The waiter is setting four glasses on the table. They're shaped like shallow triangles on long stems. The others reach out to take theirs, and I do, too.

"Chin-chin," says Bertie, raising his glass before he drinks.

Our bathing costumes reach to our elbows and knees, but all the lower part of our arms and legs are bare. Kate's costume is black, with a slashed neckline, and so is mine. Bertie and Dibs are both in blue and white stripes, very nautical.

Kate is very happy since she found Bertie. He gives her absolutely everything. He fixed the tickets for this party, and brought Dibs along to be my partner. I don't like Dibs very much, actually. He wears a monocle on a black ribbon round his neck, which looks silly with a bathing costume, and raises it to stare at people as they walk by.

"My dear," he says about a slightly plump woman, "did you ever see such a sight? Like a pregnant camel."

I wonder what he'll say about me when this is over. Best not to know, perhaps.

I take a sip of my drink and put the elegant glass back on the table. "I think I'll go for a dip," I say. But actually I want to look for Mum. I need to talk to her.

"Join you in a minute, darling," says Kate.

The clarinet player's fingers are moving quickly on the silver keys, but his eyes shift in a detached way over the people in their swimming costumes. As I pass, he lowers the instrument from his lips for a moment and blows a kiss at me.

You lookin' for the real thing, girl.

For an instant, I can smell vegetables and candyfloss.

I blush, and feel sure the hot colour of it must be spreading all over my white body.

I run across the wet tiles, drop my towel on the edge of the pool and jump in.

The water is over my head, pouring into my nose and ears. I can't swim, I'm choking, I'm going to drown. My toes touch the tiles at the bottom and I push hard against them. I'm rising again.

The rail is near enough to grab, thank goodness. I hope nobody noticed my stupid plunge. I move along to where it's shallower and rub the water out of my eyes.

When I feel a bit better I roll over as if I'm perfectly used to swimming pools and try floating on my back. It's very difficult.

"You're doing fine," someone says.

Jacoby? I flounder again, and water goes up my nose. It can't be Jacoby. Cats don't swim.

He seems dark against the dazzling lights. It's the clarinettist, it's the man in the market – no, it isn't. There's dark hair on his arms, that's all, and his hair is wet and black, falling almost into his eyes until he flicks it back.

He smiles and says, "Nice to see you."

His hand is under my back, I'm safe now, I trust him. I've let go of the bar. I want to reach up to his face and lay my finger on the sweet blue mark across his nose. But I can't see him clearly. There's water in my eyes, and the pool's reflections gallop in wild sparkles round the tiled Moorish arches, as if set spinning by a turning mirror ball.

"You want to see your mum," he says. "Of

course you do."

This is Ken, I'm sure it is.

Cats don't swim.

But the voice is Jacoby's.

I'm looking down from my bedroom window. The tin roof of the scullery sticks out into the backyard. When you're in there and it's raining, the drops hammer on it like thunder. And, from up here, through the cracked and draughty glass of the sash window, I can hear every word they're saying.

"Time you got her off your hands."

He'll be leaning against the draining board with his arms folded, watching Mum wash the tea things in the shallow stone sink.

Mum doesn't answer. Perhaps she's shaken her head.

"She's thirteen, going on fourteen, plenty old enough for domestic service," he goes on. "People are crying out for servants. Housemaids went off to work in factories in the war and never came back. Besides—"

He murmurs something I can't catch, and she gives a chuckle.

His arm will be round her, head bent to whisper in her ear. "Nice to have the place to ourselves, hmm?"

Yes, they will have it to themselves, quite soon. I've been laying my plans. All this year, I've been going round to a lady's house after school to clean knives and polish brass. When she decided I was trustworthy, she started leaving the washing up for me to do, and I scrub the floors as well, and do the ironing. She gives me sixpence a week. It's not enough for all that work, but I can say I'm experienced now. And I haven't had to ask Mum for money.

I want a live-in job, but the lady I've been working for says she can't afford a full-time servant. She dabbed her eyes with her hanky and went on about how she used to have a cook and a footman and two maids when her husband was alive. Or perhaps that's all lies and she's just a mean old cat, looking for another girl who'll do the lot for sixpence a week.

It doesn't matter. I'll look for a post elsewhere.

* * *

Mum and I are standing in the kitchen of this huge house, waiting to be sent for. I'm in my school dress and a clean pinny, and Mum found a hat I could tuck my hair into. It's miles too big for me, but she stuffed it with newspaper to make it fit better.

A footman comes in. He's wearing an olive-green uniform with gold braid on it. "Madam will see you now," he says.

His hair is very dark. It's slicked back with oil to make him look smart. There's a faint scar across the top of his nose. I think I know him from somewhere. No, I can't possibly know him. I've never been out of our village, and he doesn't live there. But he smiles at me, and I smile back.

He leads the way through a door covered with dark blue baize, and it swings shut silently behind us. We're in a hall with a carpeted staircase curving up to whatever lies above. He opens another door says, "The new housemaid, madam." He stands back to let us in. When I glance back, the door is shut and he's gone.

The room is full of bright things and soft colours. Flowered carpet, long curtains at the windows, beautiful furniture all clean and polished. The lady rises gracefully from a desk of dark wood where papers are laid out, and looks at us. Mum nudges me, and I curtsey.

"You're not very big," the lady says. "How old are you?"

"Thirteen, madam. I'll be fourteen soon." I can feel a strand of hair escaping from the hat in spite of its newspaper, and try to push it back.

She sighs faintly and says, "You'll look taller in a long skirt, I hope. And a proper cap. Sit down."

She indicates two straight-backed chairs that have been put side by side, facing her.

I perch on the edge of my chair, but as she noticed, I'm small for my age and my boots dangle above the carpet. I try to get them nearer, but Mum darts me a warning glance. *Keep still.*

The lady has put her glasses on to read the letter Mum sent. She looks over the top of them and asks Mum as though I were not there, "Her name is *what*?"

"Antigone," says Mum.

138

"Quite unsuitable for a servant." She takes her glasses off and says to me, "You'll be known here as Betty. All our housemaids are Betty. Are you used to hard work?"

"Yes, madam." I tell her what I did in my after-school job.

"And you're reliable?"

"Yes, madam. I've never missed a day."

"You're an early riser?"

"She's always in time for school," Mum says.

The lady ignores this. "Your day here begins at five-thirty in the morning," she tells me.

"Yes, madam." I mustn't look dismayed.

She's telling Mum about my uniform.

"She will need two blue dresses for morning wear, one black dress for the afternoon, and four white aprons with bibs. Plain caps for morning, frilled for afternoon, three pairs of black stockings, celluloid collars and cuffs. These things must be in a trunk, clearly labelled with her name."

"I'm sure we can manage that," Mum says.

She's holding her chin up, trying to look dignified. I can't imagine how we'll manage it.

"She will be paid fourteen pounds a year,"

the lady goes on. "After the first year, she will receive a rise of two shillings and sixpence a month." She turns to me and asks, "When is your fourteenth birthday?"

"May the eighth, madam."

"I will expect to see you on that day. Do you have any questions?"

"No, madam."

I'm trying not to grin like an idiot. Fourteen pounds a year! I'd never dreamed it would be so much.

The lady tweaks a white rope that hangs by the fireplace, and the footman enters at once. I suppose he was waiting outside.

"Alfred, show Betty and her mother out," the lady orders. "Betty is to join us in three weeks' time."

"Yes, madam."

We follow Alfred out. As we go through the baize door to the servants' quarters, he says in my ear, "It's not bad when you're used to it."

"It'll be fine," I say. I can't help grinning now, and he smiles back at me.

When I am here, I'll see him every day. I am so lucky.

*   *   *

I'm sitting beside Mum in the bus, on our way home. We're talking about uniform.

"I can make the dresses and caps," she says, "and we'll find a second-hand trunk in the market."

"I've been saving up," I tell her. "I've got nearly a pound. You can have that towards it."

I want her to smile and say that's sweet of me, but she shakes her head.

"No, you keep your money. Phil and I can manage."

We go on for a bit, up and down hills, past endless hedges.

She says, "You mustn't worry about the expense. It's well worth it. Like an apprentice buying his tools."

I nod, and stare at a passing oak tree. *Well worth it.* They'll have the house to themselves.

"Going into service is not what I had in mind for you," she adds, "but it's wonderfully secure."

I nod again.

Yes, madam.

"Tiggy? Darling?"

It's Mum.

White light.

No. Please, no.

"Sweetheart, move your fingers if you can. Just a tiny bit. Give my hand a little squeeze. Try, darling. Please try."

Fingers. No. I'm nothing. I am dark. I am pain.

"Think about wanting to try. Think, 'I want to.'"

I want to I want to I want to I want to—

The words dart about. Silver fish. They hurt.

"Make your fingers work a little bit. Think

142

about your fingers. Close them for me, sweetie.
Just a bit."

Silver fish, running down my arm, hurting.
Such a long way, miles and miles—
The fish are in my fingers.
HOT, HOT! They burn and tingle. Must
escape. Move, move—
"Tiggy! Oh, my love!"
My hand is being squeezed hard, the fish hurt
more, move again, MOVE—
"Nurse!"
There's a kind of sob.
"Nurse – look."

I've picked up a hot meat dish, damn. I dump it
on the stovetop quickly – must find a wet rag to
wrap my hand in.

I'm doing the ironing now, and my burned
fingers sting again. I'm using two flatirons, one
standing on the fire for when the other one
starts to cool. You'd think a grand house like
this might have an electric iron, but it hasn't.
There are electric lights, and there's a vacuum
cleaner that the first housemaid uses once a
week, but everything else is done by hand.

I spit on the iron to test its heat. The spit fizzles into nothing if it's very hot. Fine if the linen is well damped, but I have to be careful. I scorched a pillowcase last week because it was too dry, and the housekeeper saw the brown mark and told madam. I'm to lose four pence from my wages as a punishment.

Albert still cheers me up when he can. He's not really called Albert. That's his house name, like all us maids are called Betty – it saves the master and mistress the bother of knowing which servant is which. The housekeeper has her own name, Mrs Coker, because she's more important. And the butler is very important. He is Mr Percival.

My Albert is Kenneth. He's from Scotland, though he's learned to speak with a proper English accent. I wish I could get to know him better, but it's difficult. The benches in the servants' room are on opposite walls, and at meal times men sit on one side and women on the other, so we can't talk to each other except across the room. Kenneth stopped and said a few words to me the other day while I was cleaning silver, but Mr Percival shooed him out.

Last night I dreamed that all the servants got up from the benches and walked towards each other. The back door was open and music was playing, and we went out and danced on the lawn in the moonlight. I danced with Kenneth, under the cedar tree.

"You don't have to be a servant if you'd rather not," Jacoby remarks. "I meant you to enjoy yourself. But you wanted to see your mum, and this is where it got you."

I'm hanging out wet sheets, on a freezing cold day. I glance fearfully up at the windows of the house. Somebody could be looking.

"Don't let them see you!" I whisper.

"Don't be silly," Jacoby says. "They can't see me unless I join their game. And I'm not joining it, I'm talking to you."

That's nonsense.

"But you *have* joined it," I insist. "You're here, aren't you? There's ice on the clothes-line, look." I blow on my fingers because they are burning with the cold.

"Sorry about the fingers," Jacoby says. "It's a bit of actuality breaking through."

Do I know what he means? Perhaps I do – but he's shifted on.

"If you don't like this, you could change and be the daughter of the house instead. It might be more amusing. It would certainly be warmer."

A corner of the sheet flicks away into the wind and I grab it quickly. If it touches the grass and gets stained, it'll have to be washed again and I'll be in trouble.

"Go on, then," I tell him. "Turn me into a young lady."

And, because I am a servant and I don't believe he can, I'm laughing.

What a ridiculous sight! One of the maids is down there in the garden, hanging up wet sheets and getting in such a muddle. They're billowing about in the wind, and she's not managing at all well. She's let go of a corner, almost trips over the washing basket as she dives to catch it – ah, yes, she's got it now, she's pegging it on the line.

That's odd. She seems to be talking to someone, but there's nobody there. Perhaps she's singing to herself – I can't tell from up here

146

behind these sash windows. She's laughing now. Lucky thing, to have something to laugh at.

I envy her. I'd rather be out there in the windy garden than stuck in a stuffy room, waiting for someone to tell me what I am expected to do next.

The door opens behind me. By the firmness with which the handle is turned, I know it is Philip. I should turn round and greet him, but I won't. I'll continue to look out of the window.

"Antigone."

I'll have to face him now. I turn my head.

"Yes, Papa?" He always insists that I call him Papa, though he isn't.

"What are you doing?"

"Nothing, Papa."

"You are aware that Mr Chimberley is coming to lunch?"

"Yes, Papa."

I hate Mr Chimberley. He is boring and finicky. At lunch he'll keep dabbing at his lips with his napkin and giving me tight little smiles. His parents are rich.

"Why have you not made more effort with your appearance?" Philip demands. "That muslin dress is all very well for watercolour painting or walking in the park, but I would expect you to put on something more formal for this occasion."

I look out of the window again, but he has stepped closer. His hand is on my arm.

"Antigone, kindly do not look away when I am speaking to you. Ralph Chimberley is an extremely eligible young man, and your mother and I are very pleased that he is taking an interest in you."

"I don't like him."

"You could learn to like him. It is time you realized that you have certain duties as the daughter of this house."

His pale blue eyes are frowning into mine. His money pays for my existence. He had to take me on when he married my mother, but he can't wait to hand me over to someone else.

If I marry Ralph Chimberley, I will live in his house. I'll be mistress of my own servants, but Ralph will pay them. He will buy my clothes and everything he imagines I need. He might let me ride to hounds if I ask him nicely enough, but I will have to share his bed and give birth to his babies, and in a few years I will be too fat and matronly to ride anything but a staid old mare.

Philip is speaking again.

"Ever since your mother became my wife, Antigone, you have made no effort whatever to be welcoming towards me or even polite. Your behaviour has been consistently offensive, despite the fact that I have given you all that you could require. I feel it is time to put the cards on the table. Whether or not we like each other is immaterial. I am not asking for affection or esteem, but I think I have a right to expect good manners."

For the first time, I feel a trace of respect for him. At least he has admitted we are enemies. My head is up, and I am smiling.

"Thank you," I say.

He seems baffled by my unconcern.

"Have you understood what I am asking?"

"Yes, I have understood," I tell him. "And I agree. I will be scrupulously polite."

For once, I look straight into his pale eyes. They are pink-rimmed, weaker than I thought.

He is the first to look away.

* * *

149

I'm brushing my hair at a dressing-table with three mirrors. My maid wanted to do it – she says it is one of her duties – but I sent her away. I can't talk to Jacoby with her in the room.

"I gather you don't like this much, either," he says.

"How *can* I like it?"

I'm having a moment of seeing the game rather clearly – perhaps it's to do with the three mirrors. The two that are angled beside the main one let me see myself from the side, as though I were someone else.

"Philip keeps turning up to wreck it all," I complain. "Can't you do something about it? Tell him to leave me alone?"

Jacoby scratches under his chin. "It's a bit tricky," he says. "I mean, the man is dead, to put it bluntly. He's here full-time, same as I am. He can go where he likes."

"Well, I wish he'd go somewhere else."

"He can't do that. He's turning up because you can't get him out of your mind."

"So it's all *my* fault?"

"No," says Jacoby with his usual mildness. "He isn't anyone's fault. He just exists, that's all.

A bit like mud, really. Fine in its place, but you don't want it all over you."

He turns to lick at the fur on his back, as if sullied by the very thought.

"Mud doesn't walk into your life and change everything," I argue.

"It might," Jacoby says, "if there's enough of it."

"But how do I get *out*?"

He doesn't answer. Instead, he jumps onto the centre of the four-poster bed and digs his claws luxuriously into the quilted satin counter-pane.

"Personally, I think it's very nice here," he remarks. "However, you do have the Philip problem. Maybe you need some help."

"That's the most sensible thing you've said for weeks. Are *you* going to help? Or if not, who?"

He's thinking. "Could be your gran," he says. He's frowning a little.

"Brilliant! Can she really be here, though?"

I know I've seen Mum in the game, but Mum is almost part of me. Gran, on the other hand, seems fixed at the seaside. Perhaps it's because

I've never known her anywhere else.

Jacoby looks at me very carefully. "Don't let this worry you," he says, "but your gran will be full-time in the game quite soon now."

Something at the back of my mind says I should ask what he means, but I can't stop and think about it now. It's enough to think of having Gran around.

"That's good," Jacoby says. "And I'm sure she'll have lots of new ideas."

Gran has hired a conjuror for my birthday party. We are really too grown-up for such childish entertainments, but it's very sweet of her.

Her house is bigger than I remember it. Long curtains hang at the window, and a dark green plant in a brass pot stands at the centre. The room is cluttered with ornaments, and the green-patterned wallpaper is covered with close-packed pictures in heavy frames. It seems dark in here, despite the sparkling light from the sea outside.

My friends are looking very respectable in their long skirts and pin-tucked blouses. The ample size of Cara's bust and hips can't be disguised, but at least she's managed a well-tucked-in waistline, controlled by a wide elastic belt. Kate has a smart bow at the collar of her striped blouse, and Poppy has kept her little straw hat on, pinned at a rakish angle across her braided-up hair. Meg and Emma are here, too, and Carrie and Pam and Dorothy. We're all seated in a demure audience, facing the empty summer fireplace with its painted screen, where the conjuror is going to perform. He has brought in a long, narrow box, painted black, standing on what looks like a bench covered with a purple cloth. I feel uneasy about this box – it looks like a coffin.

Gran is sitting behind us, her back to the window in a tall chair with carved arms, presiding with amusement over this birthday treat. She is wearing a black dress with a row of small buttons down the front, and she has a lacy white cap on her head. Have I seen her in these clothes before? Somehow they surprise me. They make her seem so old.

The conjuror's reddish hair is slicked back with oil that darkens it to shiny brown, and his moustache is waxed into spikes that turn up at the corners. He's standing with the spread fingertips of both hands lightly resting on the green baize of the table's surface.

"Good afternoon, young ladies!" he cries. "Welcome to the world of magic! Who is the birthday girl, may I ask?"

Everyone giggles and turns to look at me.

"Then this charming young person shall be the first to see that there is nothing whatever up my sleeve or concealed in any way," he says. He approaches and his pale wrists shoot out of his black sleeves towards me, hands open. "Is anything there?" he asks.

"No."

I can only see the cuffs of his shirt and the dark hairs on his arms, and that's quite enough.

"Excellent." He waves a hand above my head. "Abracadabra!"

He's produced an egg, holding it high in his precise fingers. Everyone laughs. I suppose it seemed to come from my frizzy mop of hair, which everyone will now think of as a hen's nest. It appears to be an ordinary brown egg, but it might not be. Perhaps it's made of china or something. The conjuror puts it into a small basket on the card table.

Now he's dancing from chair to chair with the basket in his hand, conjuring up more eggs, one from the head of every girl. He's back at the table now, still smiling, with his fingers on the arched handle of the basket.

"And now for an old riddle," he says. "Which came first – the chicken or the egg?"

Nobody answers, of course. He flings a silky red cloth over the table, then whisks it away. The basket of eggs has gone, and, in its place, a single fluffy chick stands looking confused.

We all applaud. I have to admit, I'm perplexed. How did he manage that? Where is the basket? And where did the chick come from? It isn't a toy, it's a real, live chick, pecking unsteadily at something invisible on the green baize. I can see its long-toed feet and the brightness of its black eyes. The conjuror pops it into a battered brown suitcase under the table, and straightens up. He's showing us his empty hands, and his smile never moves.

Now he's running between us, whisking out silk scarves like a tangible rainbow. He tumbles the multicoloured pile onto the table and turns

155

it over as if looking for something.

"I can't see the yellow one," he says. "Can any of you see the yellow one?"

We all shake our heads. The conjuror looks at Poppy and says, "Young lady, would you be so good as to step forward?"

Poppy does as he asks.

"Could I ask you to remove your charming headgear?"

She unpins the little straw hat, and he lifts it gently from her head.

"Goodness!" he exclaims. "Just look what's here!" Impossibly, he pulls a wafting length of yellow silk from the hat, and bows to Poppy. "Thank you so much."

Poppy goes back to her chair, blushing.

The man conjures bunches of paper flowers from nowhere, and does amazing things with silver rings that are sometimes linked together and sometimes not. Now he's folding up the card table and whisking the suitcase aside, so that we all have a clear view of the coffin-shaped box.

"My next trick needs an assistant," he says.

He's looking at me, holding out his hand as if

inviting me to a dance. I don't want to take it, but I have to. I stand up and step forward while everyone claps and laughs. The conjuror's grip of my fingers is light and bony, very cool.

He goes to the narrow box and raises the lid, tilting it so everyone can see in. It's lined with white satin. It really does look like a coffin.

"Empty," he says. "You agree?"

Heads are nodded.

With a white-gloved hand, he is holding three swords by their tips, like a bunch of tall flowers upside down.

"I will not ask anyone to touch these. They are extremely sharp and I would hate there to be any mishap. They fit into these slots in the sides of the box. Watch carefully."

One at a time, he slides the swords in, all the way to their hilts.

"This would be impossible if anything should be in the box, yes?" he enquires. "If, for instance, a young lady should be inside it."

Everyone gasps. I stare at him in horror.

Out of the corner of his mouth, he says to me, "Don't worry – nothing will happen. You're quite safe. Trust me."

I'm as helpless as the chick on the table. I give him a small, new-hatched nod. His eyes are a tawny brown colour, and they are outlined with dark stuff to make him look more theatrical and mysterious. I will do whatever he tells me – there's no choice.

For everyone to hear, he asks, "What is your name, my dear?"

"Antigone."

"Ah." He puts his hand on his heart and bows his head in admiration. "A beautiful name. Antigone, will you help me in this trick?"

Cara gives a little shriek of alarm, but I'm saying calmly, "Yes."

"I am most obliged to you." He removes the swords and indicates the box with its raised lid. "Will you please step in and lie down? Take your time – make yourself comfortable."

He does not in fact do much about my comfort beyond bundling my skirt in round my legs so the lid will shut. "Only a few moments," he assures me quietly. "You won't feel anything, I promise."

I still seem to see his red-brown eyes as the darkness of the lid descends over me. The last thing I hear is the delighted screaming of my friends.

The box is moving, I think. Perhaps I'm just imagining it. I can't see anything in the blackness. The girls outside are still screaming. I'm trying to make myself as small as possible, knowing the sword blades must enter at any moment.

They don't come, but I'm still tense and scared, thinking they may.

Trust me. I hold on to that thought, discarding everything else until my mind seems full of those tawny eyes with the shifting points of hot light in them.

The lid has opened. He holds out his hand to me, helping me to stand up and step out of the box. All my friends are applauding madly. The conjuror kisses my hand. We both bow.

All that stuff about the conjuror was last night's dream. My head's still full of it, but it's rubbish, of course. Gran's not in a black frock and lace cap, she's sitting here at the breakfast table in her dressing gown, reading the paper over a cup of tea. This is her usual house. I've just come down the usual stairs.

She looks up and says. "Good morning! Did you sleep all right?"

"Mm." I pull out a chair and sit down. The night is still clinging round me. "I had such a funny dream."

"Oh, so did I," Gran agrees. "We were at your birthday party, but it was ages ago. All your friends had come."

I'm staring at her. This can't be true.

"There wasn't a conjuror, was there?" I try to make the question sound light.

"Yes." She's looking at me oddly. "How did you know?"

A gasp of laughter shakes me. "I dreamed it, too."

"You wanted to see your gran, that's why," Jacoby explains in my ear, "and your gran wanted to see you."

For once, I'm not listening.

"He changed a basket of eggs into a chick. Then there was a box he pushed swords through, and I had to lie down in it."

"And he found a yellow scarf in Poppy's hat," Gran agrees. "Yes?"

"Yes."

160

We're staring at each other, not laughing at all now.

"This is very odd," says Gran. She pushes her chair back. "I don't know about you, but I need some toast to help me think about it."

She goes into the little kitchen and I hear the toaster clunk down.

"Juice?" she calls.

"Yes, please."

Jacoby says, "You'd better tell her about the game. I'll leave you to it."

He's gone.

Gran puts a glass in front of me. "Apple and mango." She sits down temporarily, arms folded on the table. "So we've shared a dream. Why is that, do you suppose?"

I take a deep breath.

"Gran – this is going to sound a bit mad."

"Go on."

I tell her about Jacoby, who is my cat, but he's something more.

The toaster pops up, and Gran says, "Keep going, I can hear you from the kitchen."

I tell her, a bit louder, about the Big Dipper and the shoal of money from the gambling machine, because that's clear to me right now.

"And I've remembered something else," I go on as she brings the toast in. "You were dusting the piano. Then we set out to look at a cross-roads where there'd been a car crash."

"Does Jacoby organize all this?"

I don't know that *organize* is the word.

"He says it's a game. He plays it all the time. At least, I think he does."

I have a moment of panic. "Gran – you are *alive*, aren't you?"

"Oh, yes," she says. "At least, I feel alive, and I suppose that's what counts. Tea?"

"Please." I pass my cup.

"This shared dream," she says as she pours. "Is it part of the game, do you suppose?"

"Yes. Probably."

"Mm." She puts the teapot down and rests her chin on her hand, thinking.

"It hasn't been my game, up to now," she says. "But it has been yours. So you must have taken me into it somehow."

Jacoby is back, listening with his usual calm.

"I told you," he says. "Your gran will be full-time in the game, quite soon. This was a preliminary foray."

Shut up, I tell him silently. I'm too interested in this to listen to his ideas.

"I must admit," Gran's going on, "my mind does tend to potter off on its own these days. But I'm getting old, of course. Closer to the mystery."

"Mystery?"

"The place we go to after this one."

"You mean—"

"It's a very nice mystery." She sounds comfortable. "It's the same as the one you were in before you were born – and that was all right, wasn't it?"

"Yes, I suppose so. I don't know."

"That's what makes it a mystery. I bet it has dreams in it – they're so essential." She smiles suddenly and adds, "Don't you ever lie in bed on a Sunday morning, catching up on your dreaming? It's very important for people your age. What with school and jobs and socialising, you're dreadfully short of dream time."

Someone is banging on the door. "Are you going to lie there all day?"

Gran sighs as though she's heard it, too.

"Poor Philip," she says.

"You see?" remarks Jacoby. "I told you she'd understand. Trust me," he adds.

His eyes stare into mine. I've seen them before, tawny and outlined with black.

I shake my head. That's nonsense. Jacoby's eyes are a pale, clear yellow. They always have been.

"Your gran's going to help you," he says. "But it won't be easy."

"It won't be easy. I am a stranger to her."

There's a pressure on my hand. I know what it means. I have to make my fingers move.

I'm stronger now. I can do it.

"You see?" Mum says. "Isn't that great? Well done, darling, well done!"

Her face is close to mine, she's stroking my hair.

"Tiggy, listen," she says, "someone has come to see you. He's here, sweetheart, he's come all the way from Africa. He's going to hold your hand."

A different grasp now. Harder, more bony. Nervous.

I can't open my eyes, the light is too bright. My

eyelids are heavy, heavy. I'm trying to move them.

It's too hard. Breathe, just think about breathing.

Try again. Move—

Light floods in.

Too much. Dark again.

Breathe. Breathe.

Light. Hold on to it.

There are shapes.

A dark shape, very close.

Dark face.

Tawny eyes.

A tiger.

"Hello," the tiger says.

He has a soft voice, very warm.

"Hello, my lost girl."

10

"**G**reat party, wasn't it?" says Jacoby.

He's sprawled on the conjuror's table, surrounded by torn paper flowers. They're a wreckage of the organized bunches they used to be, and scraps of them are scattered across the floor. I think he's been playing with them.

The girls have gone home. Their chairs have been left higgledy-piggledy where we pushed them back after the conjuror had finished. Gran is sitting silently by the window in her carved, high-backed chair. She's so still that she, too, might be a thing carved of wood.

That's not the real Gran. The real Gran is eating toast in her real house. She's reading the morning paper and drinking tea – or was that a dream?

There's a bit of pink tissue between Jacoby's ears. I pick it off and smooth it between my fingers, but it stays crumpled. Yes, this is real.

"Why are you still here?" I ask.

The end of his tail flops lazily. "Why not?"

"Because – there are other things to do."

"Such as?"

I knew a moment ago, but now I can't quite remember. One thing is sure, though.

"I'm in the wrong room," I tell him. "I ought to be somewhere else."

The place with the bright lights is not much fun, as he said. It hurts. And yet—

"You keep going back," says Jacoby.

He sounds quite neutral, but I feel guilty.

"I'm not *choosing* to go back."

"I didn't say you were." He licks his paw absently. "It's just that your other self hasn't ended properly, so you're hopping to and fro. You're in between."

"In between what?"

"Between the game and the other place."

"The bright light place?"

167

"Whatever you call it."

He stretches comfortably in the pile of crumpled paper. I can see every detail of him, his paws, his whiskers and the thinner fur between his eyes and the insides of his ears. He's very real. The conjuror looked real, too, but everything he did was a trick. When I was in his silk-lined box, I was part of the trick.

Is this a trick, too? Am I in Jacoby's silk-lined game? Is he nothing but a conjuror?

My hands are over my face. I can't bear the idea.

Jacoby gets to his feet and pushes the top of his head under my hand.

"It's not a trick," he says. "All the places you've been to are real, honestly they are. The one we're in right now happens to be a dream – but it's a real dream. You shared it with your gran."

I glance across at the motionless wooden figure by the window, and feel a wave of despair. I don't understand anything.

"Jacoby, what am I to do?"

He sits down again.

"Just wait," he says. "It will happen. It already

has happened in fact, along with everything else."

"Can't you tell me what it is?"

"No," he says. "I can't see it when I'm with you."

"Why not?"

"Probably because you're still partly in the other world. But it's going to be very nice."

"Good." But I wish I could remember the other place properly.

"I can see your mind is elsewhere," he says. "You're like a moth – you have to go to the light, don't you?"

The glare crashes in. It makes a buzzing pain somewhere in my head. I shut it out again.

"Your mum can't come today, Tiggy. She has to be with your gran."

It's the voice I heard before. Warm, soft.

"Your gran's taken a bad turn, you see. Your mum can't leave her just now. She'll come tomorrow if she can."

He doesn't expect me to answer, so he goes on talking…

"She keeps hoping you'll be well and strong

again, Tiggy. I hope so, too, I'd like it such a lot. We'd get to know each other. That would be good, wouldn't it, after all this time? I never stopped thinking about you, know that? Ever since I knew you'd been born, I never stopped thinking about you."

I have to see him. The glare shines red through my closed eyes. Letting it in will hurt, but I must.

"Your gran's a fine lady," he's saying. "I like her a lot. She loves you, you know. She can't talk much since she took this turn, but she said your name. Yeah, she loves you. We all love you. Be just great if you got better and came back, you know? Be fantastic."

Pain, dazzle – hold on. Try to see.

It's coming clear. Red and white stripes. T-shirt. A dark hand, curled round mine.

My fingers clench in a hard spasm.

He stops talking. His dark face comes near.

Jacoby.

"Tiggy?" he whispers.

Not Jacoby.

Tiger eyes. Cabbage leaves. Conjuror.

Not conjuror.

Mirror.

His eyes are like mine.
I think I'm smiling.
Yes.

"All right?" asks Jacoby.

He's lying on a card table in a dark, empty room. A slit of daylight, narrow as a sword blade, strikes between the heavy curtains and shows that he's almost covered in a pile of soft, cherry-pink feathers.

I'm confused.

"I thought you were in the other place," I tell him, "holding my hand. But it must have been someone else."

"I am a cat," he points out. "Cats do not hold hands."

"No." And yet his furry softness has often wrapped me in comfort.

"So who was it?" I ask.

"I don't know. I wasn't there."

This frightens me. I thought Jacoby could be everywhere.

"Not quite," he says. "I don't belong in that life any more."

"But you used to?"

"Of course. When I was just a cat."

In the near-darkness of the room, I put my fingertips carefully on the edge of the card table. Everything has gone dangerous and uncertain.

"What are you now?" I whisper.

He stands up in a cloud of drifting feathers as light as chick-fluff, and ducks his head to rub his chin across my hand.

"I am what you made me," he says. "Half cat, half the love you felt for that cat. I am yours, Tiggy. I'll always be available. Within reason."

"But you are *yourself*, Jacoby." My voice is wobbling. "You must be real. Please say you're real."

"If you see me and touch me, then I'm real. Obviously."

"But—"

I don't want to think I made him.

"Look at it this way," he says. "I was a bog standard cat, right? An ordinary kitten, born of an ordinary cat mother."

"Not to me. You've always been special."

"That's the whole point. I was special to you. I was very lucky," he adds. "A lot of cats go through their lives without being special to anyone, so they don't have half such a nice time afterwards. Whatever I am now, it's because I became the cat you needed. And it's very enjoyable. Thank you."

"Yes, but –"

"Does it really matter that you had a hand in it?" He sounds slightly miffed. "Does it make me any *worse?*"

"No, of course not."

"Well, then."

He sounds as if there's nothing more to be said, but I'm still worried.

"Jacoby – you won't go away, will you?"

"Don't be silly. As long as you need me, I'll be here."

"Promise?"

"Promise."

The bright light place is getting to be more insistent. I don't want to keep thinking about it, but somehow I have to. If this goes on—

"I might have to be there all the time." It's a scary thought.

"Possibly," he agrees. "If you decide to."

That doesn't fit with what he said before.

"You told me all the future is already there. Like, preset."

"Correct," he agrees.

"So, if it's going to happen anyway, I don't have to decide, do I? There's no point."

"Yes, you do." He sounds definite. "The future is already there, as you say, but your deciding is part of that future. So is all the trouble you take over it. But you can't see that, so when you choose, it really is a genuine choice."

"What if I choose wrong?"

"Then you'll think afterwards, 'I made a mistake.' But that's part of the pattern, too. You can't help choosing wrong or right – you just have to learn to accept it."

My head is spinning with all this stuff, but one question stands out.

"If I go back to the other life, can you come too?"

"Mm," he says. "Difficult. I might have to appoint a substitute."

"What do you mean? I *need* you, Jacoby. *Please!*"

He's not listening. He's turned his head to look with pricked ears at the door. "There's someone out there," he says. "Waiting for you."

He jumps off the table in a billowing cloud of

pink feathers. They are falling on my hair and on my arms, and they're tickling my nose. I can hardly see through them as I follow him towards the daylight that suddenly beams in.

Gran and I are walking under cherry trees with frilly pink flowers that are shedding a cloud of petals. They're all over my arms, and they've settled in such a pile on her unravelling straw hat that she looks as if she is wearing a crazy birthday cake. We sit down on a bench under one of the trees, and Gran sighs happily.

"Isn't this nice," she says.

"This particular place?"

"The whole thing – just being here. I must admit," she adds, "it came as a surprise. I didn't expect the big change quite so soon."

She stretches out her sandalled feet, wiggling her toes in the sunshine. Her legs are slim and smooth now, with no sign of lumpy blue veins.

The cloud of petals is thinning. I shake them off my hair and rub my nose where they tickled. I'm thinking about the big change, as she calls it.

"What happened?" I ask, morbidly curious.

"What was it like?"

"I think it was what they call a stroke. I don't remember much about it, to be honest. I remember I seemed to be floating." She laughs. "Getting above myself, you might say. I was looking down at this hospital bed, with a person in it who was me."

"Oh, yes!" I know what she means. "I've done that, too! It was like being an angel."

"Nice, isn't it?"

"Lovely," I agree. "Only – I keep going back."

"And so you should," Gran says firmly. "You haven't finished what you have to do there. All the best of it is yet to come."

"But – there's Jacoby."

"He'll wait."

"Are you sure?"

"Oh, yes. He's got all the time in the world."

She looks at me and smiles, and takes my hand in hers.

The fingers closed round mine are trembling a little.

"You haven't told her, have you?" she whispers. It's Mum.

"I just said her gran took a bad turn." He's whispering, too. *"She opened her eyes and looked at me. I don't know if she understood."*

"I hope not. It could be too much."

Her fingers tighten their grasp.

"Oh, Tiggy," she says.

She is weeping.

She needs me.

It's very strange.

But nice.

"Oh, Gran," I say. "It's such a muddle."

I lean my head back and stare up at the cherry tree. Petals keep fluttering down. Pink feathers. Scraps of paper. Tricks. Illusions. Falling, coming apart, disintegrating.

"If only there was somewhere solid and reliable," I say. "Like the stone in the middle of a cherry."

That's not right. The stone is the hard thing you spit out when you've eaten the juicy flesh. Gran's nodding, though.

"A centre," she agrees.

"Yes."

"That's what your mother wants, you know.

Just the same thing."

"Does she?"

"Oh, yes. Do you remember the labyrinth?"

Labyrinth.

The word is peculiar. It's curling round and round in my mind. I know something about it, but I don't know what.

"Lawnmower," Gran prompts.

I'm an angel again, looking down from some high place to the garden below me.

Mum's pushing the clattering, old-fashioned mower round a pattern of narrow paths. I can see how it works now. Each quarter of it snakes to and fro almost to the middle, then doubles back and leads into another section. You'd have to walk through the whole design before you reached the centre.

I can see Mum's bundled-up hair with its escaping tendrils, and the back of her neck, pink with sunburn now and beaded with sweat. She's working so hard.

I wish she knew I was here.

"She thought she'd found her centre in Philip, you see," Gran goes on. "But another person can't be your centre, you have to find it in yourself."

"He gave her the labyrinth book."

"Yes, he did. He tried his best to help her." Gran sighs. "Poor Philip."

A park-keeper is walking across the grass towards us. He's wearing a dark uniform and carrying a sack. He comes close, and starts raking with long tongs in the fallen cherry petals round our feet, picking up imagined rubbish. He seems angry.

I've seen him before, this man in uniform. He's going to shout at us to put that torch out. He's close now.

"You'll have to move from here," he says. "It's a Cleansing Area. No unauthorized personnel allowed."

Gran smiles. "You're panicking, Philip," she says. "There isn't any need, you know. Not now."

The park-keeper glares at me from his hot, pale blue eyes. He takes a breath as if he is going to say something, then swings round and walks away with his sack and his tongs.

"He wants to talk to you," says Gran. "But he can't bring himself to."

I pretend to be calm. "We have talked. We've agreed that we're enemies."

"And what will that solve?"

"There isn't anything to solve."

"So you're happy to take him with you wherever you go?"

"*No*! I want to dump him, once and for all."

"In that case, you need to sort him out before you go back, or he'll be hanging around, mucking everything up."

Before I go back?

"Gran – will I have to go back soon?"

"Not very soon," she says. "And, meanwhile, I thought it might be fun to join you in your game. If you'll have me."

"Oh, brilliant!"

Jacoby is on the seat at my other side.

"Where would you like to go?" he enquires. "Or will you take pot luck?"

I think about it carefully.

"So far, I've been going further and further back, haven't I?"

"Yes," he says. "Broadly speaking."

"And it's all about how things were different then for people my age. Right?"

"Right."

"Well, if it's going to be more stuff about servants and shop assistants, I don't want to know. Isn't there a time when things were more interesting?"

"It depends on what you find interesting," he says, irritatingly.

"There weren't any shops if you go further back," Gran puts in. "Just markets and travellers with packs, carrying small goods around the countryside."

That doesn't sound much fun, either.

"Couldn't it be more exciting? Like – kings and queens and palaces?"

"No problem," says Jacoby. "But I can't guarantee who you'll find there."

I don't stop to wonder what he means.

"Come on, then! Let's go for it!"

I jump up from the bench – and find myself crouching in leaves and earth.

"My lord, I entreat you. She is still a child."

My mother sounds desperate. Crouched among the marigolds below the open window with its diamond-leaded panes, I go on listening.

Edmund is not desperate at all, merely bored.

"She is not a child. By your own admission, she became a woman two months ago. I can therefore marry her. You will not have forgotten, I hope, that I am her guardian."

"I have not forgotten, my lord."

"By the terms of my guardianship, I have the right to take her for a wife."

I can picture him only too clearly, leaning

back in his carved wooden chair and tapping his fingers on the arm. He'd hate to know I'm down here among the flowers under his window, with mud on my shoes and orange petals clinging to my skirt.

My mother tries again. "I do not dispute that right, my lord, but at least give me your word you will not rush her into motherhood. She is only twelve years old."

"Let us understand each other." He sounds tight and clipped. "I have no lust for your daughter, but her royal connections are necessary to me. If she bears me a son, by God's grace he may become the king of England. Surely you would welcome the birth of such a child?"

"Of course, but—"

Edmund sighs. "Your concerns are pointless. The law demands that I wait until she is fourteen."

"And you are a law-abiding man?"

He makes a sound of impatience. "I am a *busy* man, madam, and you have taken much of my time. I must ask you to leave me now."

My mother does not answer. I hear the swish of her heavy dress as she rises from her chair.

She will curtsey to him, and go out of the door.

"She's much better today."

The nurse brings a man from the door. He has a dark face and black, curly hair. He's sitting down beside me.

"Hi, Tiggy," he says.

I've seen him before.

"You know who this is, pet?" says the nurse. "He's your dad, come all the way from Africa. Isn't that lovely?"

I know his name, but it's hard work to remember. Yes—

Lamin.

Smiling is hard, too, but I will try.

I will …

Now he is alone in the room, Edmund might get up from his desk and look out of his window. I don't want him to see me. I'm hurrying through the marigolds to the stone path.

Jacoby's bounding ahead, as quick as a black squirrel. I'm running after him, holding my embroidered skirt clear of my feet. I hope he knows where he's going.

* * *

We're in a rose garden, shadowed by a long pergola with ramblers growing all over it. Prickly branches thick with white flowers criss-cross above our heads. Edmund can't see us in here, but Jacoby hardly slows down.

"Your gran said you'd find her in the maze," he says over his shoulder. "She likes it in there."

We come to a little paved square with a sundial in it, and run on again, under pink roses this time, and some yellow ones. Now we're out on the other side. The sun strikes down from an open sky, but there's a tall, dark hedge in front of us, with a narrow gap in it.

Jacoby runs through the gap, and I follow him. We're in a corridor of clipped yew, with leafy green walls high on either side. His black shape vanishes round the corridor's curve. I run after him, only to see him turn a corner and disappear again. The narrow strip of sky above the hedges is streaked with the flight of cawing birds. I can't look up for more than a moment, or I'll go dizzy.

"Wait for me!" I call.

"Don't panic. Slow down."

He's beside me now, and we walk on together. Every few yards, there's an opening on one side or the other, and he always knows which way to go. I would hate to be in here without Jacoby – I might wander in this place for ever.

The distance between openings is getting shorter.

"Here we are," he says.

He trots through an arch in the hedge – and we're in a small, high room with walls of leafy yew and a ceiling of sky.

Gran is sitting on a stone bench, wearing a long, blue dress and little velvet slippers. Her hands are busy with something, but she looks up and smiles.

"There you are," she says.

She's making lace. A half-completed collar as intricate as spider-web lies on a black velvet cushion on her lap, and the wooden bobbins that end each thread hang down across her blue gown. Her fingers are flicking them one over the other, as quick as someone playing a musical instrument.

"I didn't know you could do that," I say.

"Neither did I," says Gran, "but I always thought it looked very nice. You can do anything here, it's wonderful. Did you enjoy the maze?"

"Um – sort of."

A mazy kind of word is nagging at me.

Labyrinth, labyrinth—

"Ah," says Gran as if I'd spoken aloud, "now, a labyrinth is different."

"Is it?"

"Oh, yes. A labyrinth is open and helpful. Once you've set your foot on its path, it will lead you quite simply to the centre. But a maze is a kind of joke – it's meant to mislead and confuse."

"Not a very *funny* joke."

"It can be quite scary," she agrees. She pats the stone seat beside her. "Darling, come and sit down."

With her arm round me, I feel safer.

"It could be funny to the person who designed it," Jacoby puts in. "Watching the people running around in it and thinking, 'That's foxed them.'"

I don't like that idea, either.

"Isn't there a sort of secret to it?" I ask. "Like,

always take the first right and second left?"

"Some mazes do have a key," Gran agrees. "But, more often, you have to find out for yourself."

"How do you do that?"

"Just by going wrong until you get it right, I suppose. A bit like living."

Her arm isn't round my shoulder now, she's taken up the lace again. I stare at her busy hands, but I'm still seeing the hedges going past. There were places where the yew branches had been broken and the gaps were roughly mended with rope.

"People had made holes," I say.

Gran nods. "They get frantic and break through. But it doesn't do them any good. Once in a maze, you have to trust it. How do you like being a Beaufort?" she adds.

"What's that – not another puzzle?"

Gran laughs. "Margaret Beaufort. That's who you are. 1443 to 1509."

It *is* a puzzle. The numbers have no meaning. *She simply refuses to be reasonable.*

"It's a long way back," says Jacoby, as if excusing me.

An aching tiredness is making my limbs go slack. I feel as if I'd walked miles and miles through overgrown hedges as dark and threatening as a jungle. I'm wounded by its thorns and bruised by its falling branches.

Mum has come in. She's in a black coat and a black hat.

The tiger man is sitting by my bed. Lamin.

"Tiggy is so much better," he says. "She smiled at me like she really knew who I was."

Mum is pulling black gloves from her hands. She's stroking my face.

"That's wonderful," she says. "There's my clever girl."

She tries to find a smile of her own, but she is crumpled with sadness.

"How did it go?" His voice is quiet.

She moves her head in a kind of warning. She thinks I don't know what she has just come from.

I want to tell her it's all right, Gran's here.

But I can't manage words.

And this is not the here I mean.

I must do something for her.

Not just smile. Something better.
Try. Try hard.
Hard. Harder.
Touch her.
Yes.
"TIGGY!"
I can taste her tears. And yet she's laughing.

Gran and I are walking through a cemetery on the side of a hill. A river winds between the fields below us. Rooks caw in the tall trees. My jeans are damp from the long grass in the Woodland Remembrance Area. Gran is sensibly wearing wellies with her trousers tucked into them. She pauses to glance at a new stone, neat in its bed of white marble chippings, and I notice that her name is engraved on it. But that's nonsense, she's here.

I'm still puzzling over the girl I was. The girl called Margaret Beaufort.

"Gran, what *happened*? Did she marry that horrible man?"

"She had to. And he was *not* a law-abiding man. She was barely thirteen when her son was born."

"Poor thing!"

"Yes, it nearly killed her. And it didn't do Edmund any good. He died of a fever before he ever saw his son."

"Serve him right."

Jacoby has run up a tree. He seems to have some mad idea that he can catch a rook.

I stare up at him, shading my eyes against the winter sun, and ask, "Why do you keep turning me into people who have such a tough time?"

"On this occasion," he says, "it wasn't actually my fault."

"You have to blame me, darling," Gran admits. "We were talking about girls and the way they lived, if you remember. I thought of Margaret and all those royal women who had no more rights than brood mares, and felt quite cross. And it must have gone through to the game. I didn't know it would. I'm so sorry."

"That's the way it works, you see," says Jacoby from his branch. "There's no difference in the game between one time and another. As soon as a notion comes into your mind, it happens."

I'm getting a crick in my neck, looking up at him.

"Sorry," he says, and jumps down to join Gran and me.

"I'd never heard of Margaret whoever she was," he says. "But then, cats don't read books. We're not what you call educated."

"That's ridiculous, Jacoby. You know more than I do."

"That's the way you wanted me."

Gran has wandered off, looking in the grass at something that seems to interest her.

I go on arguing.

"You knew about the Cheshire Cat."

"So?"

"He's in a book called *Alice in Wonderland*. So you must be able to read, or you wouldn't have known who he is."

"Yes, I would. He's real to thousands of people – let alone being a distant cousin of mine."

"Wait a minute. Cousins are blood relatives, right?"

"Usually."

"It's not *usually*, it's *always*! Blood relatives only happen through real, living people having real, living babies. Those babies belong in families, so they grow up with relatives. But people in books aren't alive. They don't have babies."

"From what I've observed," Jacoby says politely, "they do, all the time. Look at Romeo and Juliet – I keep bumping into the pair of them, mooning around the place. They're quite young, less than twenty years since they were babies, and they belong to families, same as any couple who're alive. There's a quarrel between their respective parents, I gather. That's why everyone remembers them – that and the way they love each other."

"How do you know if you can't read?"

Jacoby sighs. "I thought you'd have under-stood by now," he says. "When someone who's not alive is real to someone who is, they belong in all time."

"But Romeo and Juliet never were alive. Shakespeare made them up. At least, I think he did."

"There's no difference. Books get real to peo-ple. Like I'm real to you. Or so you say."

"Of course you are!"

"If it hadn't been for you," he goes on, "I'd have made it here as an ordinary cat – I've seen dozens of them around – but you made me special and different, as I've told you before. If you should happen to talk to other people about me, or write about me," he adds, with a trace of smugness, "I'd get even more real. I could end up like the Cheshire Cat. Nobody bothers about who made him that way – he just *is*."

"You never explained how you are related."

"We have a common ancestor."

"But *who*, exactly?"

"She's called Old Invention."

"What's her real name?"

"That's it."

He's not being very helpful. I try again.

"When you say, 'We have a common ancestor,' who do you mean by *we*? You and me?"

"I mean the well-known cat family. Cheshire himself, of course, and Puss in Boots, and Macavity and the others from *Old Possum*, and Shere Khan in the *Jungle Book*, though he belongs with the heavy brigade. And I can't tell you how many go by the name of The Cat That Walked By Himself."

"I don't know most of those," I say.

Jacoby looks concerned. "Don't you? I hope

there are people who still do, otherwise they'll just fade away."

Gran comes to rejoin us. She's picked a whole basketful of white-domed mushrooms. She shows them to us and says, "Aren't they lovely!"

"If you like that kind of thing," says Jacoby.

It's a bit of a put-down, but she doesn't seem to mind.

"They're delicious," she says. She smiles at Jacoby and adds, "I'm new here, of course, and I haven't quite got the hang of it, but I do find your game very fascinating. Tiggy's so lucky to have you. I suppose you act as kind of tour guide, do you?"

"You could call it that."

For some reason, I sense that he doesn't like this conversation. I don't know why – he's usually so polite.

She's looking at him very deliberately. "But of course," she says, "you use a specialist adviser, don't you?"

Jacoby frowns and is suddenly interested in nibbling at a front paw.

I am uneasy.

"Who is this adviser?" I ask him. "Is it some-one I know?"

He scratches under his chin.

Fine – I'll wait.

He gives a sigh.

"Yes," he says. "I'm afraid it is."

The cemetery has gone. Jacoby and I are sitting among tall, yellow irises on a hillside that runs down to the sea.

"You have to tell me."

"This may be difficult," he says. "You don't like him much."

"Go on."

"He's allergic to cats. Not an easy person for me to work with."

"You mean Philip, don't you?"

"Yes."

"Jacoby, how *could* you?" Grief and fury come rushing up. "Don't you understand, he had you *killed.*"

"I know."

"Philip is utterly *vile*, I'll never forgive him. I've been trying to get away from him, but he keeps turning up and staring at me with those horrible pale eyes. He gives me the creeps. And all the time, you were talking to him behind my back—"

I'm in tears. Jacoby has betrayed me.

He's rubbing his head against my knees. His paws are on my shoulders, he's pushing his nose under my chin. His delicate tongue touches the tears on my cheeks.

"Don't cry," he murmurs. "Dear Tiggy, don't cry. The game would never have happened without him."

It doesn't make sense. The yellow irises are blurred with my tears.

"Just think," he goes on. "If you'd had an ordinary, happy life, just you and your mum on your own, you wouldn't have needed me so much. You'd still have loved me as your pet, but I'd never have become so special. Tiggy, do you remember? Can you get back to that time?"

It's muddled with pain and confusion, but I know he was not just a cat. He was my only friend.

"Exactly," he says. "You needed me because Philip was making things difficult. And, when he took me away from you, all you wanted was to set the clock back and make me real again. Yes?"

"Yes."

"He knows that now, Tiggy. He knows what he did to you, and he knows you haven't forgiven him. He has to live with that for ever, and he is in pain."

"Good."

"He is in what's called hell," Jacoby says. "That's how it works here. As soon as you arrive, you know about everything you did. Not the way you saw it before, but the actual truth. If it was reasonably harmless, you'll be happy – like your gran. If you have inflicted pain on anyone, you'll feel that pain yourself, as Philip does. There are people far worse than him, but he's in quite a state of suffering."

"But it won't go on for ever, will it?"

"Yes," he says steadily. "It will. That's the nature of hell. The only way for him to ease the pain is to face you. He has to tell you he regrets what he did, totally and absolutely. If he is very lucky, you may understand and forgive him."

"And if not?"

"Then he will still be in torment. And you will

go on being angry and hurt. That's a kind of hell, too."

I prop my arms on my knees, and lay my head on them. The sun is bright now, warming my bare legs and my sandalled feet. Tiredness starts to wash over me, but I fight it off.

Jacoby is watching me. "You won't be here much longer," he says.

My head comes up sharply, and I stare at him.

"What do you mean?"

"I thought at first that you'd come here to stay, but I was wrong. The other life is not ready to end yet. I can see it by the way you suddenly go tired, and get pulled back to the other place."

Small flowers are growing in the grass between the irises. Bird's eye. Speedwell. I move my fingers among them, feeling the cool moisture at their roots.

"But this is real," I whisper. "Isn't it?"

The answer is in his silence. I bury my face in my arms again. I don't want to go.

I have to choose. I can't. Not yet.

"This will wait for you," Jacoby says gently. "It's always here. Your dreams will bring you back sometimes. And when the time is right, you'll come to stay."

But there's something else. I lift my head and meet his gaze.

"What about the game? It's not finished. You said I could find something better, and I haven't. I want to go further back. There's got to be something perfect somewhere – I can't stop looking now!"

"I said you could *look* for something better," Jacoby corrects. "I don't know what your idea of perfect is. You can go on with the game – of course you can. But you need to know your time here isn't endless. That's why the question of Philip is getting more urgent."

It's hard to think about Philip without getting angry.

"What does he advise you about, anyway?" I ask. "And why did Gran have to drag the subject up? You didn't want her to, did you?"

Jacoby stretches, arching his back and digging his claws into the short grass.

"I knew you wouldn't like it," he says. "I'd have preferred her to wait a bit. But she was right, actually. She's here to help, and there's no point in letting the time drift on, it's too risky."

"Risky?"

He sits down again.

"If you went back to your other life just as hurt and furious as you were when you came here, it would all have been for nothing. That's a risk I'd rather not take."

"But do you really need Philip? Couldn't you sort it out without him?"

"No. I lost touch with you when I left your real life. When you thought of me – which was remarkably often, I'll give you that – I knew about your sadness and anger, but I couldn't see what was going on in your life. You gave me glimpses, but I wasn't actually *there*. Philip was. Until he left it and came here."

"And you thought he'd help you?" I almost laugh.

Jacoby closes his eyes in a moment of reproof, then goes on with unruffled patience.

"He has specialist knowledge, Tiggy. He knows what happened. And he has to help, if he's to get out of hell."

I can't argue round that. It's as flat and unchangeable as the straight line of the sea, pale blue beyond the hill's edge.

I give a sigh. There are some things you can't fight.

"All right – what do I have to do next?"

"Leave it with me," says Jacoby. "I'll set something up."

12

This hillside is very high above the sea, and a pattern of islands lies below me. Gannets are dropping into the silver water like stones, making rosettes that blossom and die.

I'm standing waist-deep in bracken, and sheep are moving past me along their narrow paths, snatching at the grass between the tough fronds. Although the afternoon light is still clear, the old ewe who leads the flock is heading slowly towards the sheltered, hummocky place where they spend the night. She'll stand on the biggest of the hillocks down there, watching while the ewes and lambs assemble. She never leaves that little throne-place to lie down with her own lamb until the last straggler is in.

These sheep are as familiar to me as the people who live in the low, white houses of our clachan. I know how many lambs each one has had, and whether their births were hard or easy. I know which of them will be the first to kneel down as she grazes because she has the foot rot, while others are always nimble and secure. I know which among the older ewes has started to lose her teeth, and whether she can graze well enough for a couple more lambing years. After that, we will kill her for our own food while there is still some meat on her. The lead ewe will have to go next year. She knows her reign is ending. Her eldest daughter is with her all the time now, ready to take over.

A sudden prickle runs over me. I'm not alone with the sheep – the one I've been waiting for is coming. He's still hidden behind the shoulder of the hill, but I can see him in my mind's eye. Dark hair, long, steady stride, pack on his shoulder.

My heart leaps. I would run to meet him, but the sheep might start running as well, and hurt themselves. They are nervy things, their bright minds full of wolves and eagles.

He went on the cattle drove down to the Borders a month ago. A part of me has been with him and the other men, moving with the beasts across the hills, following the old trail of hoof prints baked hard in the summer mud. I've felt his thirst, looked up into the blaze of stars as I lie beside him, wrapped in his plaid by the last of the fire. I've watched his night of drunkenness as he and the others are paid off and head for the tavern.

He won't have spent all his money. Kenneth keeps a coolness in his mind, like a sailor with an eye to the level horizon despite the pitching and tossing of the boat. Sometimes his hard ambition makes me sad. When it is time, he will walk eastward over the hills to Aberdeen, where there are books and learned men. He has to study, he says. *One day*, he told me, *women will learn, too. We are the same.*

But we are not the same. Women are tied by love and by children, by gathering peat and providing food and guarding the door against cold and strangers. I will never go to Aberdeen.

In another moment, I will see him with my real eyes. He's climbing the rise of the path.

He'll come into sight just past the windblown hawthorn tree.

He's there. He raises a hand.

There's no surprise, just gladness as the distance between us narrows.

Aaah.

In his arms I'm like a child again, rocked by a father whom I can't remember. I nuzzle into the sweet, rough smell of him like a hungry lamb.

The sheep are moving on, and we walk with them.

"You did well with the cattle."

There's no risk in saying this – his contentment makes it plain.

"Yes, the buyers liked them. So they should. We've never taken a better lot."

"That's good."

We use these words to keep a little formality between us. If we let silence blossom, I know what might happen. We could stop walking and turn to each other, and let the sheep go on. I dare not put my hand in his. My mother sees all things as I do, and she might tell Philip.

Kenneth stops, though. He has turned to face me.

"We have to be together," he says. "Don't we?"

"Yes."

He laughs. "Is it like that? So simple?"

"So simple."

I touch my finger on the bluish line that's marked his nose since he was a wee boy and got in the way of a peat spade. I slide my hand round the back of his neck and draw his mouth down to mine. Dangerous, dangerous.

No, not dangerous. My mother smiles. She won't tell.

"I'll speak to him tonight," Kenneth says. "He has to understand – we will be married."

We walk on, and now we're hand in hand.

"Squeeze my hand?"

I do as he asks.

"That's good. I'm going to shine a light in your eyes, just for a moment."

Blasts of sunlight, left then right.

"Tell me your name?"

Purple splotches from the light swim in the white sky behind his dark hair.

I've been thinking so much about words, try-

ing to find the feel of them, but it still eludes me.

"Try hard."

Antigone.

I'm trying very hard. My throat moves and a sound comes out. Now my tongue is pushing up to check it.

"Aaaa–n—"

"Marvellous," he says. "Ann will do fine. The rest will come."

I don't want to be here. I should be on the hill.

"You'll be much better soon," he promises.

We walk on, hand in hand.

Philip thumps his knee with his fist, and his pale eyes are watering with the smoke from the fire. I am crouched beside my mother as though she can protect me, though I know she won't.

Kenneth has not been invited to sit down. He stands, thumbs hooked in his belt, confronting the man who spreads fear wherever he goes.

"I will care for her," he says. "She will be safe with me."

Philip gives a bark of unamused laughter. "You forget her value as a daughter."

"I have not forgotten." Ken's voice remains

even. "But Ann is not a commodity to be traded like a bale of flax or a pen of fat lambs. She is herself. She has the right to choose."

"She has no right! She came as a young child with her mother, as a calf comes with its dam. I have fed and kept her through all these years, and you think you can walk in here and take her just as she is becoming useful? She will marry no feckless cattle drover."

"I will not always be a drover."

Philip spits in the fire, and we all hear the small hiss of it. "Easy words, boy. Any fool can delude himself with dreams. When my daughter—"

"I am not your daughter," I say, but he ignores it.

"When my daughter marries, it will be to a kinsman of my choice. This place needs a practical man, able to break new ground and clear the useless wild stuff from the hill. I have no use for dreamers." He glares up at Kenneth. "My daughter's husband will have proper respect for work and for me. As you do not."

I respect those who deserve it.

Kenneth does not speak the words, but I hear

them and glance at him with understanding. Philip sees it.

"Leave us!" he roars at me.

He's pointing at the wooden bars that rail off the other half of our small house for the cattle when they are in here for the winter. I will not go and stand there, I am not a heifer to be slapped across the rump and driven where he chooses.

Leave. Yes, I will leave, but not as he thinks.

I've scrambled up from where I crouched by the fire, I'm at the door, hauling it open. I'm running out into the moonlight.

Philip will never let me go. He will own me for ever. He will own the husband he forces on me, he will own the work I do day after day all through my life and the children I will have to bear to a man who is not Kenneth. I would rather die.

I jump the wall that keeps the sheep out of the kale patch, I'm running on up the hill towards the full moon that hangs above the cliff and the sheer drop to the sea. My mother's voice drifts after me, thin and terrified.

"Ann! Ann! Don't!"

She can see what is in my mind – the tumble of my rag-doll body through the moonlit air, turning and turning until it enters the water, making a white rosette that will so quickly vanish.

Philip is shouting too, but in anger. He's running after me, and so is Kenneth.

The footsteps stop for a moment and there's the sound of a blow. My mother screams. Philip is coming on again. I daren't look back, the ground is too treacherous. I'm jumping the deep runnels where water trickles under the thick covering of heather and rough grass. I know where these cracks in the land are, the sheep taught me each inch of this terrain, but I have to be careful.

I'm out of the heather now, running faster on the close-cropped grass. It leads all the way up to the clifftop where the world ends.

I'm at the edge.

The moon's bright path spreads across the sea far below. I am going to fall into that brightness. I'll be in the water underneath it, among dark rocks slimy with weed. Fear churns in my stomach, and a sob is rising in my throat. Ken's face fills my mind and I turn for one last look at him, but all I see is Philip coming up the slope, hands outstretched to grab me.

"Stay there!" I scream at him. "Don't take one step more!"

He stumbles to a halt.

"Ann," he gasps. For all the size and strength of him, he's not used to running. "Ann, for God's sake. *Please.*"

He's never said *please* before.

"I can choose," I tell him.

I choose to stand here. If I take one step further, I'm over the edge and falling.

Philip is imprisoned in my choosing, and he knows it. He stands there, breathing heavily, his big hands dangling at his sides. The death that threatens him will not be his, but it has him in its grip. He's as helpless as a rabbit menaced by a weasel.

Kenneth and my mother are coming up behind him. There's blood on Ken's face, black in the moonlight. My mother sees me, and puts her hand on his arm to check him.

Glancing past Philip was dangerous. I took my eye off the tiger and he might have leapt – but it's all right. He's taken a step back.

"Come away from the edge," he says. His voice sounds husky. "I won't do anything. I promise."

"I don't trust you."

I've never stared at him steadily like this before – his pale gaze has always frightened me too much. In the moonlight, I cannot see his eyes. His face is no more than a white mask, registering nothing. He lifts his hands in the ghost of a shrug. He turns and walks away down the hill.

Go after him, says Jacoby.

Why should I?

There's no answer.

Philip is distant now. He has left me to choose whether to live or die, he doesn't care. To my own puzzlement, I'm close to tears.

You didn't want him to care.

I know. But—

Everything has changed, and I don't know what to do. Kenneth and my mother are as still as the ancient stones that lean together on the moor.

They can't help you, Jacoby says. *This is all yours. But they'll wait for you.*

I take a step back from the edge. My legs are trembling.

I have chosen.

"Can you move a little more? Try moving your toes."

I'm busy, I'm too busy. I have to decide what to do.

"Try again. Try hard."

My limbs must work – I have to follow him.

"That's very good."

Leave me alone. I'm busy.

A building with a corrugated iron roof stands by itself on the empty moor. Lights shine through its high, pointed windows. I don't know what it is. A church, perhaps, or a village hall without a village. I walk round the side of it and find a porch, inside which are narrow double doors. One of them is standing ajar. It creaks as I push it open.

Books line the wooden walls of the long room inside. Down the centre runs a double row of continuous desk-spaces, facing inward but divided by a wooden screen to prevent any student from being distracted by the person sitting opposite. Each space is separated from its neighbours by a curving half-wall like those that divide horses' stalls in a stable, and each is furnished with a precisely placed chair and a hanging electric bulb in a green-painted metal shade. All the chairs are empty. There is no light apart from the double row of bright circles on the desks. Looking up, I can't see beyond the crossbeams into the shadowed roof.

Philip is leaning against a desk at the far end of the room. His arms are folded and his chin is sunk on his chest. He's wearing a shabby grey suit. He looks up when he hears me come in.

"You've come to triumph?"

His question is meaningless. Nothing has been won, so there can be no triumph. I walk towards him.

"I came because I had to." My voice sounds strangely loud in the empty room.

"You had to," he repeats bitterly. "How amazing. In all the years you lived in my house, I never knew you admit that you had to do anything."

Perhaps this is true, but there were reasons for it.

"I don't do things just because I'm ordered to."

I would do things for Kenneth freely, because I love him.

Philip picks up the words I didn't say. "You never loved me," he says with bitterness. "And, God knows, I tried."

"You took me on because I came with my mother. Part of the deal. Like a calf with its dam, as you said."

"I like to do a good job. I wanted to make a success of you."

That is probably a fact, and there's nothing I can say about it.

I ask, "What is this place?"

"The Institute," Philip says with pride. "I owe it everything."

Between the windows, there are boards with gold-lettered lists of names on them.

He raises his chin to look at one of them, like an old soldier looking at a war memorial.

"My name is there," he says. "You see?"

I don't have to look. I can see how afraid he must have been that his name would never appear on any board. That he would live and

216

die with no success and no satisfaction, value-less except to some disinterested employer.

"Something to be proud of," he says.

"Yes."

I have never liked him, but he's becoming interesting. I can see the truth of him, I can feel his feelings. Without the Institute, he'd have been nothing. He fears that people know this and despise him.

"Your mother didn't despise him, you see," Gran says.

She's knitting now. Her fingers move with certainty in the flickering candlelight. A peat fire burns in the hearth.

"He expected to be despised," she goes on. "Joy had been to a good school, she was much better educated than him. By his standards, we were well off. At least, we had been."

"Really?"

That's surprising. I always thought Gran was broke, though it never seemed to worry her. *Easy come, easy go.* Didn't she say that once, when some money came suddenly? I can't remember.

"My husband was a wealthy man," she goes on. "Your granddad. We lived in a big house with a tennis court and a lily pool."

"Yes!" A memory opens in my mind. "Mum talked about it once. I asked if we could go and see it, but she said you didn't live there any more."

"That's right. I left him, you see."

"Why?"

She shrugs. "I never should have married him. He was terribly distinguished, but much older than I was. Such a mistake."

"It doesn't sound like a mistake."

"I didn't know he'd be so old-fashioned, you see."

"Did that matter?"

She puts her knitting down in her lap.

"For a long time, it didn't. Then your mother went to Africa."

"Oh."

The memory stretches wider, and I understand.

"She met my dad. Lamin."

"That's right. When she came back, she was very quiet. Seemed preoccupied. Then one day

I found her crying, and she told me she was pregnant."

So that was my beginning. I suppose I should be grateful that she kept me.

"Her father was so angry, he told her to leave the house and never come back. So I went, too."

So simple.

But my thoughts run on. Gran gave up her husband and his big house and all that went with it. Perhaps he paid for her little place in Brighton – I don't know. To earn what she could, she gave piano lessons. My mother lived in poky rented flats, working at the library. Because of me.

Not your fault, says Jacoby.

I know. But all the same—

Gran's still talking.

"Your mum knew you can't judge people by money or the size of their houses. Things like that are luck, nothing more. Philip was the lucky one by then, but he hoped she loved him for himself, not for his money. She did, of course, but he was never sure." Gran stares into the fire. "Their best days were their last, I think, when they explored the labyrinth."

Nobody tells you when you're young that adults can be hurt. They're so controlled and well behaved, you think they're different. The more superior they are, the more you want to poke at them and find out if they're soft inside. But if you do get through, they shout and say such cutting things, you wish you hadn't. And you hate them more.

Philip's pale eyes are moist from his long staring at the lettered board. He wipes them, and looks at me again.

"If only you'd let me once think I was OK," he says.

My voice doesn't seem to be working very well and I have to give a little cough.

"Yes. See what you mean."

He doesn't move towards me, but he turns his hands palm up, still looking at me. This time it's not a shrug – it's an offer.

I step into his embrace. He's not the man I love, but it's quite good.

Ten years ago, it might have been superb.

But I didn't know.

13

"**T**ig, hi! Are you awake? It's me, Kate."

I'm dreaming. No, I'm not. It really is Kate. She's sitting on the chair beside the bed, wearing a red and white striped top.

I'm good at smiling now. She's staring at my bandaged head in some alarm.

"Wow," she says. "Looks serious."

"Yeh."

I'm getting good at talking, too.

When they change the dressings and the air comes to my head, it feels split and soggy, like a melon someone dropped. The bandages are good. They hold it safe.

"I'd have brought you some chocolates," Kate

says, "only I didn't know if I'd get to see you."

"Nn."

Chocolates would be big in my mouth. Too much.

"They wouldn't let me in before, they said only relatives. But I was coming back from shopping so I thought I'd try again. The nurse says just for a minute."

I squeeze her hand. That's easy now.

"Isn't it great about your dad!" she says. "Lamin. I bet you're thrilled."

"Yeh."

I'm not sure who she means. Someone was hugging me—

"I met him in the library. He was with your mum."

Who was hugging me?

Kate's looking worried. "Does it hurt to talk?"

"Nuh."

Everything hurts, but that's too hard to say.

The nurse is here again. Patti. On her name badge.

"Ding-ding," she says, and rings a little bell that isn't there. "Time's up."

Kate asks, "Can I come back tomorrow?"

"Course you can," says Patti. She smiles at me. "OK, Tiggy? Handle another visit?"

"Yeh."

"See you tomorrow, then," Kate says.

She waves from the door. "Take care."

My head hurts. I'm very tired.

Patti tucks the bedclothes round me.

"Quite an effort, wasn't it?" she says. "Now get some sleep."

She pulls the blinds down.

Shadow.

Green and cool.

Gran is dancing. I can see her between the pale stems of silver birch trees, moving in a grassy glade to music I can barely hear. She's wearing a white dress of silky stuff that flows with her, and the patterns she makes are beautiful, as if she's reaching out to something seen in her own mind. I watch from behind one of the trees. Its white trunk casts off curls of thin tree-skin like someone pale who's been in the hot sun. It isn't wide enough to hide me, though I'm slim. I'm worried Gran might stop if she should see me.

No, she won't notice. She is completely in the dance. The music comes more clearly now, quicksilver flutes over a rhythm of something rich and deep. She dances on, spinning and leaping, using the whole green space within its boundary of trees. I could stand here for ever, watching her.

Now she is spiralling under an upreached arm like a twisting wreath of smoke rising from a fire. Her turning slows and slows until she is quite still, one foot on its toe behind the other. The music fades to silence.

She brings her raised arm slowly down to meet the other in a melting cross that ends in relaxed hands, and moves her weight to the back foot, bowing her head as if in gratitude for something. Now she's going with a dancer's toes-first walk to a wooden bench between the birch trees. She picks up a lacy shawl, wraps herself in it and sits down.

I can't go across the green space that's been hers, it's still too magic. I skirt between the trees and come to stand beside the bench.

She glances up and smiles. After all that leaping and twisting, she's not the least bit out of breath. "Hello, darling. You've been busy, haven't you?"

I sit beside her. "Gran, I never knew you could dance."

"I always wanted to," she says. "My mother wouldn't let me do ballet classes. She said I was too fat."

"That's awful!"

"There are worse things. I can dance now, so that's fine."

"And you still play? Do you have a piano here?"

She laughs.

"Oh, yes. There's a huge Bechstein grand with a silk shawl draped over it, in a room that opens onto a garden. You can't imagine how lovely it sounds. And I can span nine notes now – I never could before. Wonderful for Brahms."

I'm glad she is happy. I won't have to worry about her when I'm – when I'm where?

"What about you, sweetheart?" she enquires. "How are things?"

"Things?"

"Philip. You did well to face him."

It's all back. The cliff, the angry man striding away down the hill. The two figures planted like stone on the empty moor.

"They'll wait for you," Jacoby remarks. "I told you. Move along a bit."

He jumps up on the bench and crouches at my side, so I'm between him and Gran.

I can still see Kenneth and my mother, frozen in their stillness. I feel as if they'll never move again.

"Something's happened," I say. "They're kind of – left behind. They weren't like that before, they were alive and doing things."

Scenes flick through my mind – swimming pool, servants' hall, sheep on a hillside – but I'm not sure of anything.

"Of course they were," says Jacoby. "You brought them with you, didn't you. So they were in your game."

He makes it sound so simple, but it isn't.

"Something's happened, though. Things are different now – aren't they?"

Gran says, "Yes, darling, they are. You're almost back in their own world, you see – the one that's real to them. They're so thrilled about it, they're not encouraging you to stay here any more."

"But – why did they come here in the first place?"

"They had to," Jacoby explains. "You were threatening to leave them. Machinery was keeping you alive – your mum knows that, although the boy doesn't yet – but the real you wasn't there. They'd have followed you to the ends of the earth to keep in touch." He smiles. "In fact, they did."

I look round at the grassy glade and the birch trees, and feel fretful.

"Why can't they stay here with me? Look how beautiful it is! Do I *have* to go back?"

"Yes," says Jacoby.

"To live your life," says Gran. "Until the next one starts."

With them on either side of me, I have to keep turning my head between the two of them as if I was watching tennis. It's a pain. Tiredness comes creeping over me, as soft and warm as bedclothes.

"Don't go!" Jacoby says quickly. "Sit on the grass, you'll see us better."

He sprawls among white daisies, and Gran sits down crosslegged with a dancer's grace.

"Your mum came here because she had to," she explains. "And the boy, as well. They are part of your web. It wasn't quite broken."

"So they were in your game," says Jacoby again.

"But why aren't they still in it?" I look round again at the green glade. "They could be here, couldn't they – but they're not."

Gran takes my hand. "At the moment, darling," she says, "you're in a game of mine."

There's a long silence. Thoughts are flicking through my mind too fast to catch – but one of them slows down, and I catch it.

"When they go back," I say a bit unsteadily, "will they know they've been here?"

"Difficult to tell," says Jacoby.

Gran gives him a reproving glance.

"They may not actually remember," she says, "but they'll understand a lot that was closed to them before. People don't come here and stay unchanged. When you've been in someone else's game, lots of new things are clear to you. Understanding is different from knowing, you see."

"How is it?"

"You can know things without understanding what they mean."

Just apply the formula.

The phrase comes back from somewhere long ago.

"And you can understand things," Jacoby agrees, "without knowing what they are." He seems pleased with this idea, but it scares me.

"I *want* to know what they are," I tell him. If I don't know, it may be I'll lose everything, plunge into the darkness. It scares me so much that I'm crying out.

It sounds very loud.

"Oh, dear," says Patti. "Did you have a dream?"

My eyes are opening, my hand is clamped hard on my bandaged head. I can still feel the noise I made. It aches in my throat.

It's all right. This is safe.

Patti takes my wrist, checking my pulse.

"Fine," she says. "I'd have been waking you up in a minute anyway. Time for another X-ray – you'll be used to that by now. And if it's all OK, we'll take the plasters off your legs and leave them off. That'll be nice, won't it?"

"Yes."

Talking is almost easy now. I'm not very quick yet, but I manage it.

Patti is coffee-brown almost like me. I'm making a question for her.

"Where – do – you come from?"

"Malaysia," she says.

She puts her foot on the lever that frees the bed's wheels and starts to push.

Someone is holding the door open. He's wearing a green overall and holds a mop. I see his face upside down as I'm wheeled by.

"Hi," he says.

He's gone.

Jacoby and I are sitting on a bench outside the back door of a house, warm in the sun.

It seems familiar. I've seen that green hose before, neatly coiled and hanging from a bracket on the wall, and the bristly bootbrush shaped like a hedgehog that stands by the back door. The garden is strange, though. It's filled from side to side with waist-high grass that smells of midsummer hay. There's a gap in front of us like the entry into a maze, and I know it will lead to a network of paths. I'd be all right, because if I stood up, I'd be tall enough to see over the top, but Jacoby might get lost in there for ever.

I hug him to me, suddenly panicked.

"What's the matter?" he enquires.

"I thought for a minute you'd gone," I tell him.

"Don't be silly. How could I?"

"I don't know."

He extends a lazy paw and stretches its claws in the sunshine, yawning hugely.

"You are ridiculous sometimes," he says.

"Sorry."

"No problem."

It's lovely, sitting here together, but there's something worrying me.

"I dreamed that everything was coming to an end," I tell him. "At least, I think it was a dream."

"It probably wasn't," he says carefully.

I know it's true. I have to leave this place.

I put my hand on his soft fur. Perhaps there's just a chance.

"Can't you come with me? *Please*?"

"I'll be around."

"But the world's so big. How will I find you?"

He turns his head to lick briefly at the fur on his shoulder.

"I don't know. It'll happen."

"That won't *do*!" I join my fingers round him and hold him up so I can look him in the eye. "Can't you see, I need to understand!"

Jacoby wriggles, and I let him sit down again.

"You can understand without knowing," he says. "I keep telling you that. Just let it happen. Humans are so peculiar," he adds. "Why do you have to make yourselves miserable over things that aren't there?

"But—"

He's not stopping to listen.

"I don't know anything. Cats never do. We understand what we need to, and that makes life comfortable, but we don't need to *know* anything. We just get on with what we're doing. Eating or dreaming or exploring – things like that. They're enough, aren't they?"

It makes me blink a bit that he lumps dreaming together with real things, but it fits with what he's always said. *If it's happening, it's real.*

But – I'm not a cat.

"I can't help it," I tell him. "Humans have to make sense of things. We need a sort of map in our heads. We have to get the picture."

Jacoby looks baffled. "Do you like all that?"

"I'm not sure. I can't imagine being without it."

"You could if you tried. Just let one thing happen, then the next. It's very simple."

I don't think it's simple at all. Or true, either.

"If you jump on the roof of the shed, you haven't *let* the jump happen," I argue. "You've *made* it happen. You've thought about it and decided you'll do it."

"No," says Jacoby, rubbing his ear in an absent sort of way.

"What do you mean, *no*?"

"If I've jumped, I've jumped. If I haven't, I haven't."

I can't believe what I'm hearing. Unless I dreamed it, this is the Jacoby who told me how time works. The Jacoby who took me through the game and let me move further and further back, living in weird places that he knew about and I didn't.

I look at him accusingly.

"You can't tell me you didn't have a mental map of the game. You must have done, it was really complicated. It still is."

"I'm glad you've noticed," he says.

"Don't be catty."

"Can't help it, can I? Being feline."

He gives me his cat grin. Oh, I do love him. I stroke him slowly, from the top of his head right to the end of his thick, fluffy tail.

"No, but really, Jacoby – there's been a kind of pattern to it, hasn't there?"

"I don't know. I just answered the questions you asked. Did what you wanted. At least, I hope I did."

I am what you made me.

"I am a cat," he says. "That's all."

"You're not, you never have been."

But I see what's happening. We're changing places. When I came here and knew nothing at all, Jacoby was my guide, my guardian angel. He had to be. Now that I'm trying so hard to make sense of it, I'm the one who's pushing for the knowledge of how it works. Perhaps I'm seeking to be my own guide. And he of course will let me do that. He will be whatever he sees I want. He will stop guiding and go back to the simplest form he has – being a cat.

I don't want that to happen. I can't bear it.

"I'm going to need you," I tell him. "I'll always need you."

His paws are on my shoulder and his whiskers rub against my cheek. I can feel him purring.

"Don't be sad," he says, and pushes his nose under my ear. "Honestly, I'll be around. You haven't seen the last of me."

"Promise?"

"Promise."

He jumps down from the bench. He walks to the gap in the tall hay, and stops to look back.

"Don't worry," he says. "I know the way."

"You mean you *understand* the way?"

He gives a purring chuckle.

"Let's say I make good guesses."

He's vanished. The hay's feathery heads move very slightly in the sun as he makes his way though its hidden passages.

* * *

"Guess what?" says Patti, beaming. "We're sending you home. You don't need twenty-four hour care now. You'll have to stay in bed for a while, but someone will pop in each day and check you over."

"Oh. Wow."

I ought to be pleased, but it's a bit alarming. I've become a hospital creature, used to bandages and medication and being loaded into a wheelchair and taken for X-rays or physiotherapy. Since they took the plasters off my broken limbs, Patti or one of the other nurses helps me have a bath. I'm always glad to get back to my home-bed for sleep until a meal comes or there's a doctors' round. I don't think I can cope in the rough world outside. I'm fragile, I need care.

"I'll miss you," I tell her.

"That's what everyone says. Hospital gets to be a habit."

A cleaning trolley is shoved through the door.

"OK to come in?" asks the young man in charge of it.

"Sure," says Patti. She smiles at me. "Here's our latest addition to the cleaning staff. You tell him if he doesn't do this room properly."

He holds the door open for her with upraised

eyebrows and a courtly bow, and she gives him a mock curtsey as she goes out.

I must be going mad. A dark-haired dream does not walk out of your sleeping brain and into your hospital room. It does not have a scar across the nose that your fingers have traced with loving enquiry. There is no reason for my heart to be pounding as if I am coming to the top of a Big Dipper, ready to hurtle down the slope.

"Hi," he says.

He starts to mop the floor, but he looks at me again and stops. His smile shifts to an incredulous laugh, as if he had opened a scrap of paper to find it's a winning lottery ticket.

"I know you," he says. "Don't I?"

"Yes." I can hardly breathe the word.

He jams the mop back in the bucket and comes closer. He pushes at the dark hair on his forehead with the palm of his rubber-gloved hand.

"Where on earth have I seen you?" he says.

I can't tell him.

A pavement at night, a half-ruined house. A clifftop.

He's remembered.

"Got it," he says. "You're the girl who was hit by a bus. You were on a bike. I was alongside you, driving a van. One minute we were all cruising along, the next, you swerved sideways."

How weird, seeing it through someone else's eyes.

"Everything screamed to a halt. You were half under the bus. I did nine-nine-nine, then I got out to look, like everyone else. A bloke got a blanket from his lorry and put it over you. The bus driver was as white as a sheet. He said, 'Control's going to send the emergency services. I don't know what's keeping them.' He kept on saying it. 'I don't know what's keeping them.' It was a hot day, but he was shivering."

"Poor man. I'm really sorry."

"Not your fault."

It was, really. But it's too late to wish it hadn't happened.

"It made me feel so useless," he says, "standing there like a prat, not knowing what to do. I went home and told the parents I was switching courses. Medicine instead of politics." He laughs. "You changed my life, you know that?"

"You're going to university this autumn."

"That's right."

"You told me. No, you didn't."

I put a hand over my face. I can't tell him what I know. Not yet.

He hasn't noticed.

"I've been doing odd jobs to make some money. Delivery driver, café work. Gardening. I like gardening. I'll keep that going in between shifts here. As a cleaner, I get a worm's eye view of the hospital. Useful if I'm going to be a medico."

He starts mopping again slowly, then stops.

"I thought I'd never forget your face," he says, "but I did, didn't I?" He spreads a hand in apology. "You look so different now. You were an awful mess on the road. Blood all over the place. I thought you were dead."

"I was, kind of. But I've come back."

He's frowning.

"I've been dreaming about you. Weird stuff. We were outside a bombed house. Must be because of the Gulf War or something."

I can't say a word.

"Then I was some sort of butler in a socking great house. And last time—"

He's leaning on the mop, staring into whatever he's seeing. I could tell him.

He shakes his head. "Stupid, isn't it."

He tackles the floor more briskly. "You never know, though. Who's to say people don't meet in their dreams? Once you kick off from reality, it's all up for grabs, isn't it?"

"Absolutely."

I want him to stop mopping. I want him to slide his hands under my shoulders and gather me into his arms. I want him to take those rubber gloves off and ruffle the short crop of hair that's starting to grow on my shaved head. I can't stop watching him as he moves round the room.

He comes across to my locker and gives the top of it a half-hearted wipe, looking at me and not at what he's doing. A get-well card falls on the floor, and he picks it up and replaces it.

"I should have sent you one of these," *he says, glancing at it.* "But I didn't know you were alive."

"Course not."

He's staring at the card again.

"Good grief," *he says.*

"What?"

240

"Your name's Antigone?"

"Yes."

"Were you were at school with my sister? Poppy?"

"Yes."

"Then – you remember me? I was two forms older."

I smile at him.

"You're Ken."

It's as though we can't stop looking.

Patti bustles in.

"You done in here?" she asks.

"Um – yes," says Ken.

"Well, get on with it. There's plenty more to do."

"Right. Sorry."

He pauses with his cleaning trolley at the door.

"Don't go away, will you?" he says.

"No. Oh – wait—"

"What?"

"Was the cat all right?"

"Cat?"

"The one that ran across the road. The one I braked for."

"I never saw a cat. If there was, it got away with it."

He's backing through the door.

"Nine lives," he says. "Like you."

He's gone.

"What was that about?" enquires Patti.

"I've just remembered it. The accident."

I'm lost.

Square buildings reach into the sky, blocking it with their ugliness. There's a flyover above me, held up by massive concrete pylons. Cars and lorries and buses roar close beside me, I'm breathing their fumes, deafened with their noise. This isn't a proper pavement, it's a steep concrete slope set with round stones so pedestrians can't walk on it. I don't know how I got here, so I can't find my way back.

I have to cross the road, but it's three lanes wide and the torrent of traffic never stops. My legs are aching because it's hard to keep my footing on this steep slope, but if I relax I'll slide down under the wheels of the traffic and be killed.

There's no way out of this place, I'm trapped

here for ever, I'm going to die here.

Traffic lights at a junction ahead are turning red. The cars are stopping. Maybe I can work my way between them and get to the other side before they start again – no, I can't. The far lane is still moving, there's a green filter letting them right. I daren't.

The door of a van is flung open.

"For God's sake," the driver says, "Get in, quickly."

It must be Ken, of course, oh, thank heaven. I'm tumbling into the battered front seat, pulling the door shut.

It isn't Ken. It's Philip, in a boiler suit and looking exasperated.

He says, "I thought we'd got things sorted."

"So did I. Haven't we?"

The lights are turning green. He jams the van into gear.

"Not quite," he says. "There's something else I meant to say. That must be why you're here."

"I didn't choose to be."

Nobody would choose such an awful place. Surely this can't be Jacoby's doing?

"Is this a different game?" I ask.

"No," says Philip grimly. "It's mine."

"But I don't want—"

"You don't want to be in my game. Fair enough. You should have concentrated on your own, then you wouldn't be."

"What do you mean?"

"You don't concentrate, Tiggy, you never did. That's what I meant to tell you. You'll never pass your exams if you keep flopping about in these daydreams."

"I don't want to pass exams."

"Yes, you do."

He glances in his wing mirror, indicates right and zooms off down a slip road. It's better here. Suburban and ugly, but at least there are some trees between the houses.

"You can't pass them all," Philip admits. "I failed a lot, specially in the early days when I didn't think I was any good. Then I found the trick of it. Concentrate on what matters to you, blow the rest."

We're leaving the town behind. It's dark now. Philip turns the headlights to full beam. A cat runs across the road ahead of us, but it's far enough away, it will be safe. If I am ever in such

244

an awful place again, I won't be scared. I'll just wait for it to end.

Perhaps my mind is wandering. I wonder what I am supposed to concentrate on.

Wait and see, says Jacoby.

All very well for him.

"No point in pushing at locked doors," says Philip. "Find one that's open a crack, then give it all you've got. The one that's opening for you now is your real life. So stick with it."

I've had about as much advice as I can take. I wish everyone would shut up and leave me alone.

Sorry, says Jacoby.

I don't mean you.

"I'm only saying it because I care," Philip explains. "I don't have much else – I never did."

We're out on the moors now, climbing up a narrow, unlit road. There's the Institute, standing by itself on the edge of the hill, I can see its row of pointed windows lit up. Philip's slowing down. He turns the van off the road and bumps it over a flinty track. He's parking by the bright windows, in the shelter of the porch.

"Haven of refuge," he says, and reaches

behind him for a briefcase in the back of the van among the lengths of pipe and plumbing tools. "I don't know what I'd do without this place."

"But – why do you keep coming here? You're a lawyer now, you don't have to go on learning things, do you?"

But if he's a lawyer, why the plumbing tools?

"Law is boring," he says. "I thought it was what I wanted, but it isn't. All those people, all those messy lives. Working too long, too hard, the constant stress of the thing. What I love is a day of practical work then coming to this place. A cup of tea in the little kitchen, then I settle down with my books and notes, and my pencil sharpener." He smiles. "No pens allowed in case some idiot marks a valuable book, that's what I call good discipline. It's the best feeling in the world, your own light over your head, a division between you and the next student, nobody to interfere or make stupid requests. Concentration, you see. No need to wonder what you'll do, you just find you're doing it. Wonderful."

So that's the game Philip made. I understand

him now. At heart, he's the same as Jacoby. *If I've jumped, I've jumped. If I haven't, I haven't.*

"Exactly," Philip says, as if I'd spoken.

We get out of the van. He doesn't bother locking it. There's nobody here, we're alone except for a multitude of stars in the dark sky.

A vertical crack of light beams out as Philip pushes the door of the Institute open. He pauses for a moment, looking back.

"By the way," he says. "I'm sorry."

He goes inside, and the door closes behind him.

14

It's only this morning that Ken was here.
Magic, magic – my mind is full of him.

Mum's here now with my lean, black father,
who smiles at me with tawny tiger eyes.

"This is so good," he says, as if he can't
believe it. "You coming home."

"Yes."

I'm almost shy of him. He's like the runners
on TV who dance about before the start line,
shaking their arms and legs. Not that he's doing
that, but he's charged with the same kind of
nervy energy. His dark hand is holding mine,
very gently.

"You know, when I first saw you," he says, "I

went back to your mum's house and cried. It seemed like I'd found you after all this time, just to watch you die."

"Well, she didn't." Mum is determined to be cheerful.

He looks at her and says, "You cried, too."

"Of course I did, who wouldn't? But she's better now, aren't you, my love?"

"Yes," I say again.

She strokes my new hair carefully, as I wanted Ken to this morning. It's growing in like black lamb's wool, but along the scar lines, it's white. Kate says it's going to set a trend.

There's so much Mum never told me. Time to know now.

"Have you kept in touch?" I ask the two of them. "Since I was born, I mean?"

"Sort of," says Lamin.

He releases my hand and sits back, looking at Mum. I can see they've talked about telling me.

She takes a deep breath.

"I ought to have done this before," she says. "But – I don't know. I felt so bad about it all. Gave you such a rotten start. Been so incompetent."

"You weren't incompetent – it was fine." I want to be encouraging.

"That's easily said," says Mum. "But anyway – the history. I went to Senegal with a girlfriend, Frances, as a sort of celebration when we finished college. My father was very against it, but my mother talked him round. I think she persuaded him I'd be living a colonial kind of life in nice hotels. But of course, it wasn't like that at all. We wanted to see the Real Africa."

Lamin gives a wry smile, but he doesn't say anything.

"When I got back, I knew I was pregnant. My father hit the roof."

"And he threw you out. Gran left him, didn't she?"

I'm not sure how I know this, but I do.

Mum looks surprised. "Did she tell you? She never said she was going to."

"Yes." I know that Gran is dead – Mum told me. But I meet her often in my dreams.

"Keeping in touch was difficult," Mum's going on. "Africa was so remote. It didn't have the things we take for granted. No phones, of course, and letters weren't much good – they

250

only got as far as the post office in the town, two hours away by bush taxi. Which isn't a taxi at all, it's a battered little minibus with no windows that doesn't start for anywhere until it's jam-full of people – and it costs money."

Lamin is nodding agreement. "It's better now," he says. "Internet cafés in the towns. There's still nothing in the country villages, though."

"No electricity." Mum's thinking back. "No water. Miles to walk in the hot dust."

"So how did you get in touch? It sounds impossible."

"I'd become friendly with a woman called Shirley Adobi. She was standing beside Frances and me at an open-air wrestling match, and we got talking. She was from Scotland – her name used to be Muir. She'd gone to Senegal on holiday, same as us, and fell in love with an African man. She went back a couple of times, then she moved out there and married him. She was a teacher. They both were."

"And my brother was the night guard at their school." Lamin is smiling, not in surprise, but because this was simply useful. Maybe that's how things work in Africa.

"So she was your connection."

Mum nods. "Yes. The school had a telephone. She'd given me the number."

I try to imagine how she felt. What had been the options.

"Did you ever think of going back there?"

"Of course I did. But I had no money. I'd blown my savings on the holiday, plus a loan from my mother that I couldn't pay back. And to be honest, I didn't know how I would cope in Africa."

"You wouldn't have done," says Lamin. "My village had no water. It was a long walk to the nearest well, and the water that came from it wasn't clean. We were used to it, but it would have killed a foreigner. There was no hospital, no doctor. All we had was rice and fish and the medicine man. It was no place for you."

I can't see how they met – the differences seem impossibly enormous.

Lamin looks at me. "I had a drum," he says. "We used to come to a thatched hut on the beach, in the evenings, to play. A few of us at first, then others would arrive, each with his drum." He smiles, remembering. "It's a different world, you know, in that music. Time goes away."

"Wonderful," says Mum. She's smiling back into her memories, and for a moment, I'm there, too. An oil lamp burning under the thatch, fast hands moving over the drums, the dark sea out there lapping on hot sand – if that's where I came from, good.

"I didn't deserve to be so lucky," Lamin says. He looks at Mum, mirroring her smile. "You changed my life."

Ken said those words to me this morning. I almost laugh, but Lamin doesn't know why.

"Seriously," he says. "Your mum paid for me to get an education, Tiggy. I'm a teacher now. Head of the primary school. The children from four villages go there."

He is so proud. His eyes are shining. I never knew what that meant before, but it's really true. Happiness is shining out of him.

How had Mum managed it? We'd been so broke until – oh, yes. I see.

"Philip."

"Of course," Mum says. "It was his money."

So simple.

We're silent for a minute. Lamin raises Mum's hand to his lips and kisses it briefly, then returns it to her lap. She covers it with her own hand, and keeps it there.

Possibilities are flying around.

"Will you be staying here?" I ask Lamin.

He shakes his head. "No. I have to go back. Tonight, in fact. My bag's in the car – your mum's going to run me to Heathrow."

"But I've only just met you!" I'm outraged.

"I know, honey," he says gently. "But I've been here five weeks – perhaps you don't know how much time has gone. Term starts next Monday. I've work to do. I have to be there."

Yes, of course he does.

"When you're strong and well, you and your mum must come over," he goes on. "I have a nice house now. Running water, electricity, computer. E-mail, all that."

"I thought we'd go out for Christmas," Mum says.

"Great."

And it is great, yes, it really is. But the emptiness is sad. My whole lifetime has slipped by without a memory that he can share. But you can't change the past. Just start again from now.

"When am I coming home?" I ask.

"Tomorrow morning," says Mum. "Isn't that wonderful? Lamin helped me move your bed downstairs, it'll be easier for you."

She's smiling, but her eyes suddenly swim with tears.

"Sorry," she says, fishing for a handkerchief. "I just – thought it would never happen."

I put my arms up and hug her.

"We're going to be all right," I say.

They've gone now, and a frantic thought is jumping in my mind.

If leave here early in the morning, I won't see Ken.

My bed's in the dining room, by the French windows that stand open to the garden. The tall evening primroses outside have floppy yellow blossoms, sweet above the dead ones. Beautiful.

I managed to walk indoors from the ambulance. They've given me crutches. I'm going to concentrate on not using the wheelchair.

Mum made tea. She gave me a chocolate biscuit, but eating it seemed hard and I couldn't finish it. Then the cup was tilting in my hand, and I barely felt Mum rescue it. I just about heard her draw the curtains against the light and creep out. I suppose the day had been quite tiring, with waiting for the ambulance and feeling agonized because Ken wouldn't know where I had gone. Then there was the journey and the difficult walk on crutches up the path that used to seem so short and easy.

I've only just woken. It was a long and dreamless sleep. Kenneth wasn't there. He isn't anywhere. I just imagined him. He's gone.

Tears are running from my eyes. I can't try to stop them or move a hand to blot them from my face, they are just happening. There's nothing I can do. There never will be.

A sound breaks through the silence. It's coming from the garden, and brings a sudden link of memory.

Mum's out there with the lawnmower again.

But it doesn't sound like the push-pull rattle

of the mower that she bought for her labyrinth. It's louder. More of a roar. It zooms close to the windows behind their closed curtains, then goes away again.

I roll over and get an elbow underneath me, and reach out to the curtain, twitch it back.

It's Philip's ride-on mower. He's going down the lawn, away from me. What does he think he's doing – he's driving it across Mum's labyrinth! Most of it's gone, there's just the pattern of its yellow loops on the flat-mown green.

A labyrinth is not a maze.

Philip is dead.

Things somersault in my mind, and I stare at the curtain clutched in my hand until they settle.

Philip is dead.

Then who—

The machine turns at the far end of the garden, by the shed where the pink rosebush blooms. It's started back towards me, felling another swathe of labyrinth.

My gasp almost stops me breathing. I'm choked with love and laughter.

He rides the mower as fast as it will go, as if

it's a motorbike, leaning it round the corners, the racing driver of the ride-on, padded knee down on the tarmac, front wheel juddering with speed. What joy.

He's roaring up the straight towards me at a flat-out four miles an hour. I raise a hand. Hi, it's me. Pit stop.

He halts the machine and gets off, leaving the engine running noisily. He comes to the French windows and puts one casual hand on the jamb. His arms under his rolled-up sleeves are sunburned brown, the same colour as mine.

"Hi," he says. "How are you feeling?"

"OK." But I'm totally breathless, and my heart is chattering like a two-stroke engine.

I manage to ask, "How did you find me?"

"Happy accident," he says. "You know I said I was doing gardening?"

"Yes."

"I had a phone message, asked if I could tackle a lawn that was overgrown." He grins. "Overgrown? Positively agricultural."

I can't believe this. "And it was Mum?"

"Yep."

Why isn't he more surprised? He just looks pleased.

"When Patti said you'd gone home, I asked her where you lived, so I could keep in touch. And it was the same address as the lawn I had to mow. Useful, huh? But talk about dead weird. There's something going on, if you ask me."

We look at each other and laugh, because it's so crazy. But I'm worried about the mowing.

"The overgrown bit – it's Mum's labyrinth. Does she know—"

"Oh, yes. She said to mow it flat. She still wants to do it, she says, but grass doesn't work. I said she wants a weedproof membrane first, then maybe gravel or recycled glass. There's lots of things you can do with that stuff. Hang on," he adds. "I'll turn this mower off. Planet-wrecking emissions and all that."

He silences the machine, then leans in at the French windows again.

"I've got something for you."

"Have you? What?"

I hope it isn't chocolates. Somehow they still seem too thick and heavy.

"You know you were talking about a cat?" he

says. "One that was on the road? Well, I just thought—"

He stoops beside the evening primroses and picks up a cardboard box. He brings it in and puts it on my bed, pulling the string undone.

A small black kitten is scrambling out. His eyes are still blue and his little tail is pointed at the end like a Christmas tree. He nuzzles into my hands as if he's home again.

Ken's looking anxious.

"I hope this is all right," he says. "Patti told me she'd heard you talking about a cat in your sleep. Jacoby, you called him. She told your mum, and your mum explained what had happened. She was really worried that it was upsetting you. Our cat had kittens and this one was left, so—" He shrugs. "I can take him back if you'd rather not."

The kitten is vibrating with a ridiculously big purr. I tuck all of his little self into the hollow between my shoulder and my ear, and reach my other hand up to slide it round Ken's neck and bring him close.

My bedside lamp is lit and the curtains are

drawn. The French windows are shut. The garden with its shaven labyrinth lies outside in the dark.

Mum provided the kitten with a litter tray and a box with a warm blanket in it, but he swarmed up the bedclothes and settled on my pillow.

Tomorrow, I'll send a card to the bus garage, for the driver who ran over me. Just to tell him I'm all right and say I'm sorry. A first job, back in the real world.

I reach for the bedside light, and switch it off.

Told you I'd be around.

The kitten's name is going to be Albert.

"From the stars you can tell time and distance and you can find your way home. As long as you know them, you will never be lost."

Najmah has always been told this by her father. But caught between the Taliban and American bombs, she is both lost and alone.

Over the mountains, in Pakistan, Elaine is waiting for her doctor husband to return from the war. She also looks to the stars, praying that somewhere he is alive and gazing up at them too.

As Najmah and Elaine search the skies for their answers, their fates intertwine – under the persimmon tree.

"Don't cry. We won't be parted, I promise."

It is 1662 and England is reeling from the after-effects of civil war, with its clashes of faith and culture.

Seventeen-year-old Will returns home after completing his studies to begin an apprenticeship arranged by his wealthy father.

Susanna, a young Quaker girl, leaves her family to become a servant in the same town.

Theirs is a story that speaks across the centuries, telling of love and the struggle to stay true to what is most important – in spite of parents, society, and even the law.

But is the love between Will and Susanna strong enough to survive – no matter what?